]

THE UNDEAD SITUATION

"As people turn into monsters, a monster learns how to be human.... The zombie apocalypse meets its match in sociopathic survivalist Cyrus V. Sinclair, the antihero of Eloise J. Knapp's *The Undead Situation*."

—Craig DiLouie, author of *The Infection*

"An action packed trip through the 'zombocalypse' with a unique character as our guide. Eloise J. Knapp has delivered very strong entry to the genre and I can't wait to see what she comes up with next. Highly recommended."

—Timothy W. Long, author of *Among the Living*

"A roller coaster ride through terrifying and sometimes disastrous events… Knapp has managed to introduce some fresh new scenarios into her zombie tale with some unexpected turns."

—ZombiesDrule.com

"I enjoyed this novel so much more that I expected to … Once I started, though, I found it hard to put down. I am really looking forward to reading more from this budding new author."

—Red Adept Reviews

THE UNDEAD SITUATION

Eloise J. Knapp

Permuted Press
The formula has been changed...
Shifted... Altered... Twisted.
www.permutedpress.com

Acknowledgments

All streets, cities, and roads are geographically accurate. Some liberties have been taken with the creation of various buildings and the aesthetics of certain locations.

Sam Landstrom, my uncle and author of *Metagame*, inspired me to finish my own novel after completing his.

I'd like to thank the earliest editors of *The Undead Situation*: Alanna Belak, Laura Landstrom, and Angela Berg.

A PERMUTED PRESS book
published by arrangement with the author
ISBN-13: 978-1-934861-58-5
ISBN-10: 1-934861-58-8

Well, it happened.

When it did happen, everything about it was cinematic. I'm sure people banded together and tried to save themselves from their untimely dooms. They found solace in a mall, a house, or bunker, just like in the movies. Desperation and pessimism just prevented them from seeing the film-like qualities of their actions.

I was sitting in my apartment, alone, when it happened. Downstairs I could hear the banging of pots and pans as people fixed dinner. Their kids were whining, but that wasn't anything unusual.

Outside the sky was plagued with deep grey clouds, rain pouring. I left the window open so I could hear the softness of it.

A train whistled across town. A cop car, sirens blaring, sped past the front of my apartment building. I listened to its sound fade away, again leaving me with the noises of my home and of rain.

It happened all at once, taking the entire world by storm. It happened so quickly, people didn't believe it was true. Denial just made the undead count rise alarmingly fast. People who accepted it were considered crazy by those who didn't. In the end, I bet everyone wished they'd seen a few more Romero movies, maybe been a little less close minded.

If I were to try and tell you exactly how the whole zombie thing spread, I'd probably have to make up some stuff. No one knew if it was a disease or infection, or why it also made you turn when you died from non-Z related injuries. Oh, experts—especially religious experts—had a jolly good time with their theories, but no one truly knew what was going on. So, as I sat alone in my apartment, the chaos-inducing news of the zombies finally spread to Seattle, Washington.

People died then they came back. They ate other people. It's a cliché way of putting it, but it's the absolute truth.

There was only one person I knew who would accept the news as quickly as me—my long time friend Francis. He called early on with the latest update on the situation outside.

"You're supposed to quarantine anyone who's been bit, did you know that?"

"I hadn't heard."

"Boy, don't you turn on the TV?"

"You know I don't have a TV."

The apocalypse *was* now, and since Frank and I were alike we both accepted that without much thought. I wasn't sure what Frank's plan was, but I got out my box of old Guns & Ammo for entertainment, barricaded my apartment door, and cracked open a can of sweetened condensed milk for the ride. (I've got a sweet tooth. Sue me.)

With my canned goods obscene in calories and a top-story view of Seattle, I watched people die. I watched stuff blow up, stuff break, and the zombies gain numbers for their undead ranks.

My name is Cyrus V. Sinclair, and I didn't care.

Chapter 1

I wasn't going to leave.

I was going to leave.

Only days after the outbreak started, downtown Seattle was in a state of chaos and disrepair. From my window I watched people from all walks of life, all shapes and sizes, and of all colors get eaten by their fellow man. Some people thought zombie movies were graphic, but nothing was as stunning as watching the action in real life.

Really, I suppose everyone's intestines tasted the same. Discrimination wasn't an issue once you were a zombie.

A fully loaded military grade pack waited by the front door. When I packed it, I had intentions to leave. That was when rumors of the dead rising started. Now the dead *had* risen and I was still sitting in my apartment, hesitant to make a decision. Just one decision. But instead of deciding, I was thinking about the world outside.

I decided we were all doomed for sure, and maybe that's why I hadn't stepped outside of my apartment in almost two weeks. Before, there was a chance of survival; the military was still trying to get control of things, the electricity was always on, and most people were still acting like…like people. But once the lights started flickering and occasionally went out, casting the whole city into complete suppressive darkness, I knew it would be just me, myself, and I 'til the end of days. My ferret, Pickle, was my only companion who would accompany me for the apocalypse. For days we shared comfortable silence, eating gummy bears and ferret food, watching the mass destruction of mankind unfold before us.

The monotonous days were broken up by phone calls from Frank. My cell vibrated on the kitchen counter. He spoke before I could even say hello.

"How bad is it there?"

I didn't have a TV, internet, or interaction with other people, so my personal opinion was limited. "Not too bad. The power's still on, plumbing works mostly, and apparently I get reception."

Frank huffed. "Well, I'll *tell* you how bad it is. The coast is overrun. No ships coming in or out. A man going east told me he saw freighters ramming into shore. Goes without saying everyone is killing each other, living or dead. Damn government said they're taking appropriate measures."

It was surprising how fast civilization fell apart. One minute we were haughty Americans, the next we were as bad off as every other human being on planet Earth. Despite the government's claims they could save everyone, or they were taking "appropriate measures," people went berserk and the world went straight to Hell.

"Doesn't matter what everyone else is doing. I'm fine here," I said.

"You're still in the apartment? How long are you planning on staying there?"

How was I supposed to know? One minute I was ready to walk out the door, and the next I was ready to hole up in the apartment forever. "I don't plan on staying here. I've been thinking about leaving."

"Well, lucky for you, you don't have to think about it anymore. I'm coming to get you."

I masked a gasp with a choke. Keeping my voice level, I asked, "What are you talking about? I thought you were still in Little Rock?"

Frank, in few words, explained that I couldn't take care of myself worth a damn and he was going to pick me up. His parents, survivalists like Francis, left him a cabin in the mountains which he'd been working on for the past year. That meant Frank had been in Washington for a year without coming to see me. I felt a little hurt, but didn't mention it.

"I'm not the same teenager who showed up on your doorstep, Frank. I can handle myself."

The static of the phone almost masked it, but I heard him snort in disbelief. "Never said you were. So you're saying no to the cabin?"

I knew I wasn't thinking it through, but pride overtook me. Frank was an honorable man, and he was only looking out for me. But I couldn't stand the idea of someone thinking I couldn't take care of myself. I just couldn't.

"That's right. I've got a plan and I'm sticking to it."

"You've got a plan? You just said yo—"

The cell made a horrific high pitched squeal before going silent. No automated voice explained the phenomenon.

That was the last time I used a phone.

* * *

A few days after talking to Frank, I regretted my decision. His intention was noble and I shot him down. Our conversation was probably our last, and I acted like a complete ass. My pack was still resting by the door, and I visualized it mocking me for saying no. Then the bag reminded me of how I met Francis. I was sobered by the thought.

In 1993, when I was 16, my grandparents and I had just moved to Little Rock, Arkansas. At that point I was 'just too far gone.' The epitome of a no-good punk. Unwanted, I packed my few belongings and ran away. I wasn't smart and didn't know the area, so I unintentionally hiked up into the Ozarks.

I found myself on the property of Francis Jackson Bordeaux with a shotgun pointed at me. Frank was a Vietnam veteran with a mean case of Post Traumatic Stress Disorder.

Long story short, I lived with him for about a year until I moved onto another chapter of my life. I learned a lot from Francis J. Bordeaux, almost everything that mattered.

I thought about Frank's personality, how when I lived with him and I said no, he took no as yes every time. A part of me believed, despite my harsh refusal, he was still coming to get me.

He was, I decided. There was no way he'd changed enough *not* to come get me. That was when my plan was set; I would turtle up in my apartment until Frank came. Until then, it was the same old routine. Watch outside, maintain inside.

Frank opened my eyes to how bad things were in the city. Instead of just looking, I analyzed the situation. The entire city was clearly on its way to complete destruction. Looters took advantage of the turmoil and broke into every shop they could. Even the windows of the children's toy store across the street were shattered, dollies and teddy bears strewn everywhere.

Despite not leaving the apartment (or maybe because of it), my body was still fresh and lithe. I hadn't spent a single day running away from animated corpses or fighting my way through hordes of the living trying to escape to a different fate. At twenty-seven, I was as spry as any teenager, maybe even more so. (Undoubtedly, my laidback personality had something to do with it.)

As I walked through my two-bedroom one-bath residence, I took mental note of its state. The kitchen and dining room were both sparsely furnished. Someone would think an inhabitant was nonexistent. The short hallway and bedrooms were stark, void of any personal expression. The only signs of human existence were empty canned goods on the kitchen counter, an H&K PSG-1 towering among the empty bags of candy in the dining room, and a scatter of Frank Sinatra records resting on the living room floor with the record player.

There were many places I'm sure I could have gone to get some goods. There was a convenience store down the street that offered all the candy I could eat. (One might wonder how it's possible for me to live on sugar. The answer was this: I don't.) My bedroom overflowed with MRE's (Meals Ready to Eat), the flavorful choice of the U.S. military. Although their flavor wasn't as delicious as a roll of Life-Savers, it kept me running.

Call me crazy, but I knew some kind of apocalypse would happen in my lifetime. I wasn't necessarily preparing for the undead, but stocking up on MREs over time seemed like a good idea anyway. Stockpiling gun after gun since I was sixteen? Well, that was just a hobby.

After moseying into the eating area, checking what I did have left food-wise, I went back to the balcony to assess the corpse situation. The spring air was impregnated with the stench of rotting flesh, a scent not unbearably unpleasant, and within that the electric undertone of a lightning storm soon to come. The street had emptied. I guessed the dead had better luck indoors, where people might still be hiding, so they went hunting inside.

A mom and pop grocery store stood across the street from my building, next to the book store. It looked thoroughly looted. Windows were nonexistent and rotting corpses lay on the ground. I figured there had to be some sweets still available in there, though. Who went for things like candy when the mindless dead were seeking them out? No one, of course, but I got grouchy without a good sugar fix. I was also bored and wanted to leave.

Even though the streets looked abandoned, there was no way the undead weren't waiting in the shadows for lunch to come strolling by. I'd have to be cautious.

A simple backpack would suffice for raiding. It was big enough to hold a lot, but wouldn't get too heavy and weigh me down. After a thorough search of my apartment, I dug up a crowbar to use as a silent melee weapon. I was taking my 9mm, not because I was trigger happy but because it was necessary. Despite my abundance of ammo, using the gun would only draw more attention. A gun shot was a dinner bell; one I didn't want to ring.

Weeks had passed since I had last left the apartment. I wasn't sure I could step out of it without being eaten alive by the pesky undead. But I had to try.

After unlocking the three deadbolts and removing the extra wooden plank across my door, I peeked out. The hallway was scattered with random junk and the walls were smeared with dried blood. Only one or two of the apartments were open. Down the hallway was an elevator next to emergency stairs. The elevator was partially closed, with half a corpse wedged between its doors. The door to the stairs was closed.

When I passed the open doors, I shut them as quietly as possible. I wasn't sure if zombies could open doors, but it wouldn't hurt to close them. One of the rooms revealed a man, an undead bag of skin and bones, who had apparently hanged himself early on. His throat was torn up, but he still tried to groan in relief at the sight of me. He swayed as he tried to come after me, overwhelmed that a meal finally stumbled his way. The rope was Kevlar, a material he'd often expressed fondness for. Between the quality of the rope and his barely existent weight, I wasn't surprised he was still hanging.

His name was Rick Johnson, I remembered, as I stared at his face. Years ago, when I moved into the apartment, he tried desperately to invite me to dinner to meet his daughter. My lack of interest ended in a fight, after which we never spoke to one another again. That suited me just fine.

I shut that door, writing Rick and that story off all together.

Except for a dull thudding noise behind Apartment 8's door, the creaking of Hang-Man's rope, everything was quiet. The silence was ominous, especially when I considered what horrors lay behind the closed doors. My mind ramped up with thoughts of ghouls eating themselves as a last resort, or just standing around in the rooms forever, or at least until someone came and killed them.

My luck held, and I made it down the flights of stairs without incident. The main and only entrance to the apartment wasn't broken in any way, but why would it be? There wasn't really anything to loot in here. Someone would have to be desperate to raid a low-class apartment building like mine.

Before I left the lobby downstairs, I studied the street from my new ground view. Paper and dark blood coated the sidewalks and the street. I could barely make out the asphalt from all the debris. There were body parts everywhere. Half a torso here, an arm there. One lower half still twitched, but since it couldn't do me any harm, I didn't care.

The carnage was interesting to look at—in a modern art kind of way—but I didn't want to spend too much time surveying. This mission was a run in run out kind of deal. No matter how long I waited, or how hard I looked, they'd still be there.

Slowly, I pushed the door open and slipped through, glancing up and down the street. A single zombie stumbled out of a clothing boutique, but hadn't noticed me yet.

His arms were gone, with only a few scraggly tendons and nerves left dangling from sockets. A hideous smashing of skin, bone, and muscle made up his face. I doubted he could even see, so I took advantage of his oblivion and made a dash across the street.

My boots slapped against the ground and echoed loudly. It couldn't be prevented, but the noise made me cringe. Running was a zombie's second favorite noise. It meant breakfast, lunch, or dinner. Maybe all three. (A Zs favorite noise was people screaming—that generally meant he got lucky.)

The grocery smelled foul before I even went inside. A thick scent bombarded me, choking me as it hit in waves. It wasn't just the smell of rotting food. A body I had spotted earlier was slimy and covered in maggots. This one had been dead for a considerably long time and was extra gooey. (I never knew organs took on such bizarre colors when rotted.)

With my back pressed against the wall, I turned and peered through the corner of the broken window. I couldn't spot any Zs above the short aisles, but they could be crawling or crouched too low for me to see. The whole place was the poster child of an apocalypse. Only a few items remained on the shelves. Rotting dairy products had turned green after falling from the refrigerators. There was a puddle of curdled green goop just beyond the doorway. I tried to breathe through my mouth and not acknowledge the stench.

Without thinking twice, I jogged into the store, stepping carefully as to avoid the wet patches on the ground. I shrugged my pack off and unzipped it, keen on shoving in as many goodies as possible. The candy section was practically untouched, save for a lone arm rotting near Snickers bars.

Glancing around, I pilfered Life Savers and listened intently for any zombies. A soft squeaking caught my attention as I stuffed Hostess cupcakes and Twinkies in the top of my backpack. As the squeaking grew louder, my pilfering sped up.

A torso pulled its way along the floor. It was a woman, once, but I could only tell because of her chest. Her hair had come off in clumps, leaving behind a ragged, bloody skull. Her face had been scoured off, leaving nothing but tattered gore behind. White, foggy eyes bulged out of her skull. Intestines followed behind her, creating bloody trails on the checkered linoleum floor.

I was quiet. Didn't move a muscle. A slick pool of blood in front of her hindered her progress. Torso Woman ground her teeth in frustration and let out a loud, teetering groan as her arms thrashed about.

Somewhere outside a chorus of replies sounded off, reverberating down the street and into the store. My position had been given away. In a world infested with undead, if there were two entrances, then there was only one exit. The one you came in by would be the one zombies filed in through. For me that meant no exits. My luck with the immobile Torso Woman would run out once other, more capable zombies saw me.

After I zipped and secured the backpack, I approached the woman and killed her with one swift whack from my crowbar. I went to the entrance and took the risk of running straight out.

The armless zombie was steps away from me. I darted past him, scanning the street as I went. Behind him another two followed. To my other side, multiple Zs were staggering out of storefronts, excited by Torso Woman's call.

My apartment was just a walk across the street. If I ran fast enough, I'd be able to shoot right by them without taking time to put them out of their misery. I took that option.

Gnarled hands grabbed at me as I barreled through, wrenching the door open the moment I was close enough. There was no time to lock it since they were right behind me, salivating for my flesh. Adrenaline carried me up the stairs faster than a hunted rabbit.

As I entered the hallway to my apartment, a zombie lunged from the side. My sidestep would've worked if there hadn't been a sour patch of blood and other coagulated liquids resting on the maroon linoleum where my boot struck. Instead, I slipped and fell onto my back, the undead going right with me. His ridged hands clawed at me while he snapped his jaws at my exposed neck. Crowbar long forgotten, I reached into my holster for the 9mm while I held the pus laden beast away. With one burst of strength, I knocked him off and brought up the gun simultaneously, squeezing a bullet into his head. Grabbing the crowbar and holstering the handgun, I scrambled to my feet and rushed down the hallway. All the apartment doors I shut remained shut, except for mine which I had left open.

How could I have done something that dimwitted? I wanted to take my time and check the rooms, but couldn't risk the delay, so I walked straight in, slamming the door shut. After quickly locking the bolts and dropping the extra board into position, I stood still and listened, already questioning my decision to lock up so early. But I'd rather fight one or two Zs trapped inside than the horde coming from outside.

No noises gave away an undead, but that didn't mean one wasn't there. Crowbar on the ready, I glimpsed into my spare room. It was empty, as was the bathroom next to it. Leaning the other way, I took a step forward, glancing into my bedroom. It, too, was clear.

I went to the end of the hall, which opened up into the living area, and stopped cold. In the corner of the room, near my records, a woman swayed back and forth, facing the wall. Adorned in a tweed business suit with minor rips and stains, she appeared relatively normal. Her hair was still up in a tight bun, revealing mottled gray skin. The only giveaway was a bullet wound through the back of her neck.

She turned around slowly then caught sight of me. Her on switch triggered, she lurched forward, trying to close the distance between us. I took a step down the hall and watched as she stumbled, almost losing her footing. With steady hands, I gripped the crowbar and raised it above my head, waiting for her to stand up.

I brought the curved end down, lodging it into the top of her head. She snarled and gnashed her teeth at me, trying to move forward, but I held her at bay with the crowbar. It didn't go in deep enough to actually kill her, but it kept her at a safe distance.

Thick brown liquid dribbled down her chin as she swung her arms out. I pushed her back, using the crowbar as leverage, until we were both on the balcony. Good thing I left the sliding glass door open.

Cracking indicated her skullcap was going to give way. I pushed her until she was at the edge of the railing, gave the crowbar a quick tug, releasing it and a chunk of bone. Before she had the chance to lunge at me, I gave her a hard kick in the chest, knocking her back, sailing down to the hard asphalt below. Her body landed at an odd angle and the back of her skull exploded. Safe at last, I tapped the crowbar on the railing until the piece of skull and hair fell off.

Inside, I dumped out my backpack on the dining room table. Candy scattered everywhere, and I sorted it by level of deliciousness, like a little kid on Halloween.

Mission accomplished.

* * *

I stopped keeping track after awhile. What was the point in keeping track of days when you didn't have anything to do? No appointments, no dates, no work. Nothing. I didn't have a calendar to begin with, so it didn't matter. (Actually, now that I think about it, I didn't have obligations before either. Only nowadays, I couldn't leave the apartment if I wanted to. That was really the only difference of pre-apocalyptic life for me.)

Resources were not an issue. The city water had stopped flowing a long time ago, but water was easy enough to collect. I set every container possible outside to catch rain, which worked out well since I lived in Washington. I transferred full containers to the bathtub whenever possible.

Entertainment was an issue. Guns & Ammo didn't amuse forever, which forced me to search the apartment for something else to do. There were a couple boxes of my old college books, so I set to work on those.

I read them all, then I read them again. If I had that kind of determination while in college, I might've stuck around. But I didn't, and I don't regret it. The apocalypse made me a smarter person. I wonder if the same could be said about other survivors.

(Ah, the history of college…Instead of finishing my degree in pharmacy, I found a buddy who forged an entire background for me. I got all the benefits of having the degree, without the work or debt. The whole idea seemed clever to me, and landed me jobs in drugstores.)

After I finished reading all those college books, I understood physics. My mind grasped how a light year worked, and I could recount the evolutionary history of man in a heartbeat. Even the lighter books were appealing, like art history or geography. If the world was ever rebuilt, I'd be one hell of a commodity.

For now, however, book smarts were useless at the end of an apocalypse day, so when I wasn't reading, I was building my strength. If I let my body deteriorate, I'd definitely regret that. Every day I'd do as many exercises as I could remember, then I'd make up a couple.

* * *

Neighbors have books, I realized one afternoon, upon finishing my fifth Guns & Ammo collage. Boredom often invoked irrational actions, and seeking literature in insecure rooms fell into the "irrational" category. But since my level of boredom was high, I ventured into the unlocked apartments, hauling out as many books as I could.

I avoided Apartment 8 and Rick's place. No need to see him again. The thumping was relentless.

My book stock refreshed, I set to work. Even the kids' books were appealing. Who knew Nancy Drew had it in her to solve so many mysteries? I had a good thirty or so of those, courtesy of a little girl's room in 7, and read every one of them twice.

In time, desperation for entertainment even forced me to read through a mind-numbing trilogy called Twilight. Apparently there was a fourth one, but I was not interested in trekking down to Barnes & Noble for it.

* * *

How did I get Pickle?

Let's start with this: the average lifespan of a ferret is about seven years. For personal reasons, two years prior to Judgment Day, I decided I needed to get a pet. Seven years seemed reasonable, seeing that it wasn't too long, but long enough to gain some life experience.

So, on March 9th, I found myself in a pet store looking at albino ferrets. Much to my chagrin, they were fresh out of normal ferrets, but hey, I'm not racist. I appreciate all breeds.

After I brought the tiny girl home, we found ourselves quick companions. She wasn't afraid of me, appeared to love me despite my strange habits and unusual personality. She was the perfect woman. She didn't ask questions. Or speak. Or take up space. Like I said, the perfect woman.

* * *

Sometimes I wondered how other people were handling the end of the world. I doubted most people took things the way I did. (Over the years, I decided my apathy about the whole thing probably meant I was an anomaly, and I came to terms with that.)

Early in the crisis, my undead neighbors had left their televisions on maximum volume. My sound-proofed walls could barely buffer the nonstop noise, since it was coming from below and both sides of me. If it wasn't for the power outages, I would've gone crazy. Francis would call, wanting to discuss the latest on the undead situation. He told me the experts were debating constantly over whether the undead were human, or if they retained memories or some of their personality when they turned.

"I reckon they don't, Cyrus."

"I don't think so either. People need to stop fantasizing and get real."

"Dead *is* dead."

I scoffed at some of the earlier attempts to quarantine the living dead to study them, find a cure, and make things okay. There was no cure. This was it. The end. Didn't anyone understand that? The walking dead were walking dead, and they didn't have an ounce of anything human in them anymore.

Every zombie out there was probably a loved one at some point. People who didn't want to put a bullet in their loved one's head were the instigators of the problem, in my opinion. If everyone saw things for what they were, there wouldn't be a problem.

I imagined the survivors of the initial outbreak hovelling in offices, homes. They were alone, and it must have been driving them mad. What I enjoyed as solitude, they probably thought was mind numbing horror.

They had no food, no water, and no weapons. Most likely, they were slowly dying, fearing an animated corpse would consuming them soon.

The differences between them and me were astronomical. I was alive because I wasn't like other people. If I were, I'd be one of those men who wished he weren't alone during his last leg of existence.

If I were one of those men, I'd be dead.

* * *

I mused over my lack of fear toward the living dead. While lounging on the floor of the living room, gnawing on a protein bar, I wondered why I couldn't muster up an ounce of anxiety.

The undead were terrifying. At least, they should be. I'd seen so many of them, falling apart and ghoulish. They chomped their crusty, blood-rimmed mouths and thick, strange liquids came out. Some of their stomachs were so distended from gorging on human flesh they exploded, leaving organs and entrails hanging like jewelry.

Their collective stench was putrid. At the very least, I should have felt nauseous when the breezes from Puget Sound carried their scent through my opened windows.

Upon finishing the bland protein bar, I crawled over to the dining room table, reaching up for candy. My hand returned with a bright orange, rectangular package. I made my way back to the living room and collapsed onto the spot my body had warmed.

As I savored the two Reese's Peanut Butter Cups, Pickle slinked down the hall and over to me. I caught her beady red eyes looking at me.

"How about you? What's your position on all of this?"

She climbed up my shoulder and onto my chest, where she perched righteously and eyed my candy. The rodent had a taste for candy, which I occasionally indulged. Being the terrible pet owner I was, I let her have a quick nibble before popping the rest of the chocolate in my mouth.

Some things never changed. Her sense of entitlement was one of them.

Chapter 2

My peace, uninterrupted for so long, was abruptly broken. Rapid firing of an MP5 came from behind the AM/PM down the street. It was unusual to hear gunfire these days. My attention captured, I leaned against the railing of my balcony and watched as a tactical-gear-clad figure bolted around the corner of the building.

I couldn't determine a gender; but no woman could've made it this far by herself, so I decided to think of it as a 'he.' The man stopped after a couple of yards and looked around for threats. Another gust of wind steered through the street, kicking up paper around him.

Occupying the end of the T-shaped road was the AM/PM, and from either side of it shuffled packs of zombies, undoubtedly lured by the seductive sound of gunfire. The MP5 let loose again, but without aim, so the ammo was wasted. Turning, the shooter ran down the T with a great burst of stamina I admired. The living dead joined their flanking attacks together to form one column. Some of them moved faster than the others, breaking clear from the slower ones.

They must be eager, I thought.

While they made their slow and steady advance to lunch, the man made like a rabbit and raced down the street, undaunted by the weight of his supplies. Soon he stood underneath my balcony, looking up. I could see the shiny reflection of the world around him in the visor of his helmet. And then I realized 'he' was a 'she.'

The woman ripped off her riot helmet to reveal a shaved head, but her face had youthful, pretty curves. Not like I cared. I just noted it, was all.

"Help me!"

I chuckled, amused she was speaking to me, amused that a woman was running around bald, with a gun.

"Why? You seem to have a good grasp on the situation."

She shoved another magazine of ammo into the gun, pointed it at me. My smile faded.

The pending storm I prophesized had arrived. Rain trickled at first, but turned into a downpour quickly, drenching her and me both. Still, she refused to look away, even as fat droplets of water found their way into her eyes.

"Help me or I'll shoot that fucking smirk right off your fucking face!"

Clenching my jaw, irritated by the fact that someone, a woman no less, was telling me what to do, I raised my hand and pointed down the street. A good twenty walking dead made their way toward her. The woman abandoned her request for help, running to the front of my apartment building, flinging the front doors open. I hoped she'd stall long enough for the Zs to get her. It would've been a phenomenal sight to see someone so fiery try and knock off so many zombies. But that fantasy was shot down once she disappeared into my building.

Through my DIY soundproofed walls, I strained to listen for her, debating whether or not to let her in. I wasn't a sociable man, so having company would actually be a downer. I wasn't a defenseless man, so having her join me wouldn't necessarily improve my defenses. At any rate, it didn't take long before I decided if she made it here, she clearly was a human worth living, male or female. Not long after my decision was made, I heard the dull sound of suppressed gunfire through my door. The girl had switched to a revolver. Moments later she was frantically kicking the entrance to my haven.

"Open the door!"

Without further hesitation, I did.

She glanced at me before stepping in. How blindly trusting, but I supposed if I were normal and the threat of death were impending, I would be trusting, too.

"Shut the door."

"But you wanted it open so badly," I mocked.

Pointing her little gun at me wiped the smile off my face. After I locked the deadbolts and pulled over the heavy piece of wood that served as extra protection, I turned on her. No one pointed a gun at me twice and got away with it without some kind of retribution.

She had turned her back on me to look in the living room. Quiet as a snake, I came up behind her, grabbing one arm and twisting it around her back. The gun in her right hand dropped, making a small thud as it hit the grey carpet. I twisted harder and harder 'til she screamed in pain and dropped to one knee. Pressing my mouth against her ear, smelling damp skin and sweat, I whispered, "How does it feel knowing I could kill you right now?"

"It doesn't feel any different than the past five days, bitch."

I wanted to kill her for her insolence. I had killed people before. Not many, but even one was unusual compared to normal standards. After being harassed so much in high school (by the bullies who were conflicted on the inside, or so their parents said), I'd strangled one in the woods behind the school. Nicky was my second kill, and when it happened I was unfazed by what I had done. All I felt was relief from not having to deal with bloody noses and black eyes anymore.

This girl, though…this one's spunk was growing on me. I released her and she sat on the floor, panting. Standing my ground, I rolled my neck around a few times, cracking it.

"You've been here less than five minutes and you're already stressing me out."

"You didn't have to let me in."

"If I hadn't, you would've shot me." A lie, for I could've easily evaded her bullet.

"Sure."

I laughed and gave her my hand, offering amends. She took it and I hoisted up her light body.

"I'm Cyrus V. Sinclair." The narcissist within me enjoyed the way my name rolled from my tongue.

"I'm Gabriella. What does the V stand for?"

"Virtuous."

"You're fucking kidding me."

"It was a virtuous act saving you."

We stood there in heavy silence until I, unaffected by social awkwardness, went into the living room to look out the window.

"We can't stay here," she said from behind me. "They'll get in. They always do."

"I don't think so."

"I do think so. What makes you think here is safer than anywhere else?"

She was damp from head to toe and shaking. Across her back was a pack with a shotgun protruding. Her MP5 was slung across her shoulder and dangled at her side. The only skin revealed was some of her neck and her head. Everything else was covered by military gear. Who in the hell was she?

I scolded myself for this burst of curiosity over a woman, or anyone for that matter. I'm not exactly popular with women. Why, with having no sex drive or fantasies, I was hormonally blank. Please, call me asexual.

"My door, my apartment. They're extremely safe," I explained. "Besides, I'm waiting for someone."

"A door? I've seen them come through door after door. Yours isn't any different. Waiting for someone? Whoever they are, they're probably dead."

"My walls are insulated. My door is custom-made, trust me. The zombies go by sound, but they cannot hear us. They also go by sight. As for smell? I suppose they could smell us out, but I'm very sanitary." I looked at her. "I suppose you should clean yourself up."

Gabriella bit her pouting bottom lip and shook her head in true defeat. "I guess if you say so. You've been here since it started, so it must be true."

"It is."

"You'll have to leave eventually."

Keeping my body shielded from the view of any undead below, I moved to the side of the windows and peered outside. The dead were dispersing from the street, but it appeared some had found their way into the building.

"I told you. I'm waiting for someone. I'll leave when he gets here."

"Waiting for someone? What dimension are you living in? He's probably dead."

Returning my gaze to her, I ran my tongue over my teeth absentmindedly. The previous silence I had been living in was ruined—by the zombies moaning, her breathing, and Pickle's frantic running behind objects to hide from a stranger. Exhausted by it all, I heaved a sigh. It was best to ignore her comment before we started fighting.

I told her I'd get her dry clothes, but she said she had some in her backpack. After I pointed her to the hall leading to the bedrooms and bath, she vanished for an hour. By the time she got back the sky was dark, thunder rumbling through the lifeless city. Rain lulled me into a sleepy state as I lay on the living room floor.

"I'm sorry for what I said," Gabe whispered. "About your friend being dead."

"It's fine. It isn't unreasonable to think that. But I'm still waiting for him. You can do what you want."

Dropping the subject, she leaned against the wall. "What do we do now? Share stories of better times?"

I laughed, low. "These are my better times, baby."

Chapter 3

"At school, my sister claimed zombies would be real some day. I didn't listen to her, of course. Who the fuck would, right? Embarrassing."

Gabe often tried to bring up normal life, but I found it awkward, and the conversation never progressed beyond an "oh" or "yeah" from me and ensuing silence from her. This time, when she brought up her sister, I didn't dismiss her quite as fast.

My sister never claimed zombies would be real, but she said a lot of other strange things. Ivy never spoke a word to anyone but me, and when she did she told high tales so convincingly, sometimes I thought they were true. Her favorite theory was that two small men lived under our house, each coming up only to slap her once and take mayonnaise from the fridge. To deter the villains, she methodically buried new mayo and rinsed the container until the smell was gone.

I never said a word to our grandparents about what Ivy said or did, so they had no clue what kind of mental state she was in, which was for the best.

It wasn't as though I didn't care about her. I did and still do. But I knew our grandparents would force her into therapy, just like they did to me when I was even younger than she. If I did one good thing for Ivy, it would be to keep quiet about her abnormalities.

Thinking of my sister left me feeling weighed down and listless. What I felt must've been tangible, because Gabe started off down the hall, perhaps picking up on my change of mood.

My favorite boredom spot was the middle of the living room floor, which is where she always moseyed to when she was interested in conversation. I was alone again, waiting for her return. This time she took her time in coming back, but came back nevertheless.

"I'm sorry."

"You're forgiven," I said, figuring she knew she'd hit a sensitive spot.

Gabe sat next to me, a little too close, and set a hand on my shoulder. I stiffened, but didn't move away. *She isn't coming onto you*, I reassured myself, *just trying to comfort you.*

"My sister was hard to deal with. My parents said she had Asperger's Syndrome. It made it really hard for her to talk to people, but when she did she said stuff like that. She was just...awkward."

I wasn't sure why she was telling me this, but for some odd reason I felt comforted. Hesitant, I said, "There was something wrong with my sister when we were kids. She's normal now."

She pulled her hand away and stood up. "I wish I'd listened to her. Not about the zombie thing, but about *everything*. She was the only sister I had and now she's gone."

An unfamiliar tightness in my chest started, and my eyes felt hot. I didn't respond, knowing if I did I might cry.

Crying was a sign of weakness. To make sure I never got that close to it again, I took to lying around my bedroom, door shut, instead. She couldn't make me cry if she never saw me.

* * *

Gabriella worried. It was natural at this point in the game, but my opinion of her declined because of her insecurity. At first the battle-hardened youngster didn't mind staring at a wall for hours. Without stress, she would sleep away the nighttime and sunlight hours. She was a cool cat, but after a few days she became as jittery as a nervous horse.

(I hate horses. No zombie apocalypse could ever change that.)

A few days after her arrival she asked me what was going to happen. We hadn't spoken even a page of dialogue, and the question was one requiring a novelette to answer. I shrugged. That spoke volumes.

Gabriella worried, but I didn't. At the onset of her insecurities I began to wonder why I didn't care like she did. Why, with each passing day, she grew more and more sullen, while I remained flat lined in the emotional department. Was it because she coasted on a level of humanity I couldn't get to? Or was it because I was on a higher level of being? One that didn't require humanity or anything parallel to it?

"What were you going to do? Before you decided to wait for your friend."

The question itself seemed void of real emotion or curiosity. It was raw but sterile. I wondered why she was even asking if she held no interest. But I'd never been good at reading people. No zombie apocalypse would ever change that either.

"In reference to what?"

"All this." She waved her hands to emphasize the nonexistent concept. "What were you going to do about the zombies? This isn't a movie. It's not like you're going to find a mall and camp out. You're not going to get on a boat and sail away, and you certainly aren't going to Rambo it."

Gabe, as I had come to call her, was sitting on the kitchen counter staring at me. I felt unsettled.

"Why do you care?"

"I don't."

"Why did you ask then?"

"I don't know."

Time clicked away our lives as we sat in silence, simply looking at one another.

"I was going to wait for them to all rot and fall apart."

She raised an eyebrow. "The whole world?"

"I wouldn't have to worry about the whole world. Just this general side of the U.S."

"That would take a long time," she said, seeking flaws in my plan.

"Time never was an issue for me. It isn't for anyone now."

She rolled her eyes, which was her way of agreeing or admitting defeat. "Then what would you do? After they were rotted and gone? There would be no one left."

I grunted. "I've lived for ten years without the world. It doesn't need me. I don't need it."

Her laugh was bubbly and out of place in the situation. It disturbed me. How could I be the source of such amusement? I almost looked for a secondary cause.

"You're such an old man. A hermit. What then? Once you have the whole world to yourself?"

"I'd keep on dying like I am now, until I died. Only difference is I wouldn't have to be as social as right now."

She clenched her jaw, rage evidently too intense to remain suppressed. Removing herself from the counter, she stood facing me, hands flexing in and out of fists. I stood up, accepting her challenge.

"It's always been people like you who fuck our world over. People like you who don't give a damn about anyone but yourselves!"

Her shouting made me edgy. My soundproofing stopped the undead from hearing, but that didn't make me feel better. I didn't want to have any part of whatever emotional baggage she was unpacking on me.

"You act as though I'm the one who has issues," I said. "In reality, I'm the one who's still living peacefully. Excuse me, who lived peacefully until you showed up."

Gabe didn't move an inch as I walked towards her, face contorting with spite for something still unknown to me.

Closer yet I moved, one small step after another, closing the seven feet between us. I gambled farther into my speech, knowing it would distract her from my catlike advance.

"I believe I saved you. I believe you are also extremely ungrateful."

Six feet.

"Your soul-tormenting issues probably pile higher than the world's current body count, alive or dead. Right, Gabe?"

Five feet.

"You're jealous I don't have the petty attachments to normal life like you do."

Four feet, my voice lowered.

"You're jealous of my freedom, my ability to be so cynical without any guilt."

Three feet. My voice was a husky whisper.

"You want the life I have. The life of a recluse who can do whatever he wants, whenever he wants, even in this chaos."

At two feet away, I loomed over the small teenager. She tilted her head to keep eye contact, still holding her vow of silence. I leaned closer, stealing away the space that gave her false protection.

"And worst of all—for you—is you know I'm right."

When silence still greeted me, I became angry. I wanted a response and she wasn't giving me one. She dredged up old, painful memories every day. She made me *feel* things I didn't want to feel, remember things I did not want to remember. I abhorred domestic violence, so I wasn't sure why I did what I did next. I grabbed her by the shoulders and slammed my head against hers.

She screamed in pain and fell to the floor. Unhurt by the head-butt, I dropped to my knees and grabbed her calves as she tried to flip onto her other side and scramble away. Pulling her closer to me was effortless, as was my goal to entrap her. Before I scored, she managed to bring her knees up and kick out, hitting the center of my chest. I wasn't expecting it. Air burst from my lungs as I fell backwards, head connecting with the dining room table before meeting the ground. A searing hot pain flashed in my head, and my vision became foggy.

Gabe got up and prepared to take advantage of my position. She succeeded with a poor kick. As her boot joined my kidney, I grabbed her ankle and twisted hard enough to hurt, but not hard enough to break. She yelped and lost her balance, while I held fast to her sprained ankle.

In control again, I twisted around until I could grab her other foot and knock her to the ground. I climbed on top of her, returning her cheap kick with an equally dishonorable punch. Blood burst from her mouth, droplets splattering onto my otherwise clean carpet.

With my free hand I grabbed at my belt, pulling it from its loops.

I realized I had been screaming at her the whole time, but I hadn't been paying attention to the words flying from my mouth. She was screaming too, but I didn't care what she had to say.

The belt went around her hands, just as a temporary binding until I could get something better. I yanked at it, eliciting another scream from her as it tightened and ripped at her flesh.

"What to do, what to do, what to do," I said, dragging my hostage from the kitchen to my bedroom. My muscles strained from the effort.

I smiled at Gabe. In return, she let off a string of profanities followed by a projectile of saliva. Unfazed by her insanity, I flung the closet open and pulled out a ring of black cord.

After much fighting, much yelling and hitting—a bloody nose for her and a split lip for me—I bound her wrists in front of her.

Our final moments before I threw her off the balcony were very pleasant.

"I hope you burn in hell, you motherfucker!"

"We'll burn together, baby."

* * *

Gabe fell two and a half stories down. Dangling from the black cord I held, she bounced a few times. So I changed tactic and slowly lowered her. Only a few Zs were on the street, but the louder we were the more they would come.

The balconies weren't directly under one another. Below mine was brick wall, but to the right was another balcony. It was far enough away Gabe couldn't get to it, close enough to remain an idol of false hope for her. But I knew it was unrealistic to leave her hanging by the wrists for very long. Loss of blood circulation could cause the loss of limbs and other maladies. I shifted the rope far enough to the side so the tips of her boots rested on the lower balcony, easing the strain on her wrists. But she could still smell the rotting corpses and see the fine details of their decomposition, which was what counted.

Her little episode forced me to take action, to discipline her. The new world, the world after the zombies, wouldn't tolerate her kind. If and when Earth recovered from the walking dead, the survivors would be the cold and heartless.

Who was I kidding? I didn't like Gabe, but that's not why I lost it. She was too much my opposite. She felt too many things and made me second guess myself and remember the person I used to be. Hell, she even made me remember a toy train I got for Christmas when I was seven. But I had to keep up the act. I had to pretend I was a sociopath, since I couldn't reverse what I'd done.

"See what happens when you have outbursts?" I called down.

She flailed, slipping on the railing before settling once again. Stopping, she looked up at me. A raw, bright streak of blood washed down her mouth and chin.

"Let me back up!"

Laughing, I shook my head and proceeded to tie the cord securely to the metal railing in front of me.

"Why?"

"Simple, you dick! The longer I stay here, the more of those things will come. They'll climb on top of each other until they can reach your damn safe haven."

Her point was farfetched. It held a smidge of validity, but I didn't care. I wouldn't be able to stay there forever, as much as I would've liked to.

"I suppose they'll get you first, seeing how you're down there," I stretched my arms above my head, groaning at the pleasant feeling of muscles working, wincing at the pain in my chest and abdomen, "and Pickle and I are up here."

Metallic, putrid scents wafted upward. Across from me, a freakishly obese man walked onto his balcony. His arm was out if its socket, hanging on by a thread, and coagulated blood soaked his left side. Even a complete idiot would be able to tell he was dead, what with the vacant white eyes and moaning.

I motioned to Mr. Chunk and the zombies gathered below her. "I guess I'd better leave you to the party. I never was one for parties. Too social for my liking."

Gabe's eyes were frantic and bulging. She hyperventilated, but I knew she wouldn't die from it. Just a panic attack.

As I walked back into the apartment, I heard the first of her long, hysterical screams. I forced myself to become the apathetic monster I always tried to be.

Chapter 4

I was a little boy once. I had a boyish physique and long, messy red hair. Trucks, trains, and the outdoors were the staple activities of my life. Finding a stick and hitting things with it was prime time fun for little old me.

In fact, I had parents once, too. When I was young, our parents died in a boating incident, leaving me and my sister orphans. If I remember correctly, she was devastated by their deaths. I didn't know why since they never spoke to one another.

My grandparents gladly took the place of our deceased creators, shipping us off to Alabama to live with them. They were kind, as grandparents should be. My grandfather smoked a pipe and read the newspaper. He drank his coffee black. My grandmother was matronly and an avid Bible reader. She read me and my sister stories. Made us oatmeal cookies on Saturdays.

The rest of my childhood was arguably idyllic—almost sickeningly so—which brings up one vital question: how could it have produced me? I am a fellow of great intelligence and philosophical bent. However, I do have an affinity for violence and destruction. Humanity is a trait I lack, but was one my grandparents had in abundance.

Why couldn't my kindhearted grandparents rub off on me? Whether it was because of my parents' death or being the sole communicator with my disturbed sister, I don't know.

My first kill was only months after moving to Alabama. It was my eighth birthday, and the grandparents were throwing me a party. I had no friends, but they managed to invite kids from church and school. In the pool, after everyone left, the two remaining kids wrestled me out of my lifejacket. The pool was too deep for me and I couldn't swim well, but neither could they.

I grabbed one of them, the smaller one, and took him down with me. I used him to push myself out of the water for a breath before going under again. We kept it up for only a short time before he stopped moving and someone pulled me out of the water.

From the outside, it looked like we were both drowning. An accident. One of the moms pulled me out while another dad went in for the dead boy, no one blaming either of us. It happened so fast. No one was looking.

Only I knew it wasn't an accident.

Maybe that was what changed me forever. It seemed like a traumatic enough event to fuck me up permanently, but I'm not quite sure.

It must have been the realization that the world was a horrible place filled with horrible people who would never amount to anything. It was filled to the brim with people who were apathetic and money driven, with no real goal but to get more money. To live more indolently or to have a bigger TV. Yes, that must have been it. When I saw the majority was flawed, I wrote off trying to be like them. The kids taking my lifejacket was a metaphor for how I saw the whole planet.

The undead situation shook everything up. No one cared anymore about bad people, goals, or indulgences. We were all on equal ground, and that made things interesting.

In fact, I dare say it made living worthwhile.

* * *

Spring wasn't planning on giving way to summer. It was probably mid-June by now and it was still cold. Through steel-toed boots and thick wool socks, I felt thoroughly chilled. I was wedged into the corner of my bed, which was pressed to a wall, curled up against the sounds of rain outside. Since Gabe arrived, it rained constantly, the liquid varying in severity, but relentless nonetheless. Such weather wasn't uncommon, but I couldn't stop myself from making foolish correlations between her and it.

When I had nothing to do, I thought. Recollections of a childhood, consciously repressed, rushed back to me for no apparent reason. Sometimes I thought the memories were significant, but most of them were mundane. Me riding a bike to school, or one of Grandma's old church friend's scolding me.

Drip, drip, drop. Drip, drip, drop.

From somewhere in the house came the maddening metronome of dripping water. It drove me insane. I would've gotten up to find the source, but what if I couldn't find its location? I'd grow even more insane, endlessly searching. In the end, it was easier not to bother.

Isolation made me nostalgic and dizzy, most often with a feeling of stagnation. When I felt like that, thinking about my past was the only entertainment, even if said entertainment was odd.

Pulling the blanket closer, I sighed. Life was a nonstop run for me, so I never paused to mull over my past, present, or future. But why would I? There was nothing in that dark closet that would change anything about me. Reminiscing was nothing more than dredging up old, insignificant memories.

Boredom knew exactly how to leash me and lead me, nudging me into cynical thoughts and life-questioning dilemmas. No matter how hard I tried to keep my mind blank, I kept returning to how my life really was going to be, especially now that Gabe was around. No one ever mentioned meeting up with another survivor.

Drip, drip, drop. Drip, drip, drop.

Overlaying the beat of the water-metronome were Gabe's moans, and the moans of zombies outside. They provided the bass clef melody to the song of my meaningless thoughts.

Pickle rifled through the candy on the dining room table. Soon, a soft thud signaled she had abandoned the cause. Minutes later she was in the middle of the doorway to my room, staring at me. I brought my hand out from the covers and beckoned her, only to have her scamper off out of sight.

Gabe had been hanging outside for only an hour or so. Already masses of undead clambered beneath her, eyes filled with blank, empty hunger. For the first twenty minutes, she screamed until her throat was raw. The she went quiet, then back to her grousing. I began to reconsider my actions, but never for very long. I couldn't change the past, so why think about it?

Drip, drip, drop. Drip, drip—

"Cyrus!"

The scream startled me. I turned my neck too fast, sending hot pain up it and into my head. The tips of my fingers flew to my neck, rubbing up and down the hurt nerve, seeking reprieve.

"Cyrus! Quick!"

This scream was different. It didn't possess the pathetic tone of a plea, but the loudness of authority, not to mention a dash of lunacy.

Kicking the cold comforter from my body, I rolled out of the bed and scrambled to the balcony, tripping multiple times. Pickle went berserk from my fast, clumsy motions, and took to running around the living room in a blind panic.

Outside was just as cold as inside. Rain beat down from the sky. The drops were even and dense, cool and refreshing. I tilted my head back into it before another shout snapped me from my daze.

"I've learned my lesson, Master. Please, bring me up."

Gabe looked up at me, smiling. Her teeth were stained an unpleasant tint of pink, her chin and nose dark with dried blood. Cleansing rainfall hadn't washed her clean yet. A pitiable laugh escaped her.

"Why are you smiling? You don't have anything to be smiling about."

"When life sucks the fuck out of you, you just gotta grin and bear it, right? I get it… You're the head of the pack. I'll go by your rules. It's not like I haven't done that before."

I rubbed my face, slick with rain, and screwed my eyes shut. It stung keeping them closed, but I welcomed the searing pain.

Guess I'd done as much damage as I could, leaving her there. Maybe I broke her psychologically. When I decided to bring her up, it wasn't an act of compassion, but one of pride.

Once she was at the top, I hauled her over the railing. We went back inside as though nothing had happened.

Once settled in, I listened for the water drops that had threatened to take my sanity.

They were gone.

Chapter 5

If fate were paying attention and wanted to make things cinematic, the rain would have stopped when I let Gabe back in, representing the cliché of a new beginning. The sun would have come out, the zombies would have all died, and we would have repopulated the earth with battle-ready mini-Cyruses.

I might have said this before, but life isn't a movie.

Also, Gabe was too young for me, and didn't have appropriate genetics for breeding.

I helped her hobble back into the apartment, while the continuous storm grew angrier, blowing with all its might. Rain beat down on the roof so hard we could hear it through the wind and rumbling thunder.

I brought her into the bedroom and allowed her to lie on my bed. Picking up the abused comforter from its resting place, I placed it over her, awkwardly. I was no mother, no caring father. I didn't know how to console the dying or aid the sick.

Clearing my throat, I looked out the window—a distraction from the situation at hand. The sight that greeted me was no better. A little girl stared back from the building next door. Tiny, bloody hands clawed at her shut window, white eyes gazing at me hungrily. I tugged at the cord on the blinds until they gave way, shutting the disturbing image from Gabe's view.

"Why did you do that to me?" Gabe's hoarse voice barely stood out from the howling wind outside. "Never mind. I don't care. It's over now. I don't have anywhere safe to go."

It's over now? Who says? I realized Gabe handled the entire me throwing her off a balcony thing a bit too lightly. This brought into question her past, and what she was doing before she came to me. If she were hiding something from me, it would certainly make sense to grit her teeth and bear my lunacy.

Maybe she wasn't the tough girl she made herself out to be. She did say she didn't have anywhere else to go, and in a world like this… Well, I imagined a person could put up with a lot if it meant they weren't being eaten alive.

It wasn't going to be safe here for long. We'd be able to stay inside the apartment for as long as we wanted, but eventually we'd have to leave for supplies. There might be too many of them to even do that. The word "trapped" sprung into my mind.

You're not safe and it's your fault, I thought. While easy to blame Gabe for being loud and drawing Zs, my actions were what caused the developing problem. How could I have been so careless and let my anger take control? Every minute, another handful of stiffs were coming around the corner because I lost my cool. Any chance of safely escaping the apartment had vanished.

I clenched my jaw and stopped scolding myself. What happened happened. Nothing I could do about.

Then there was Francis. I wanted to wait for him, of course, but it was becoming less rational by the day. If there was one person I was willing to wait for, that I wanted to fight the apocalypse with, it was Francis Bordeaux. Gabe showing up distracted me for a while, but now my mind was back on Frank. Was he coming? Should I even bother waiting?

Gabe mentioning somewhere safe to stay challenged my notion of how safe I really was. I thought of the little girl next door, vacant face staring into the room, or the mass of undead gathering below. I thought of my one friend in the world and wondered how safe he was.

Keeping Gabe in my apartment was the second most human thing I'd done in my life. The first being the fifteen days I spent in the Peace Corps. Helping people for nothing in return except gratitude didn't work for me. I thought it would be a 'life changing' experience like the testimonials said. After that I gave up on being normal.

A sinking feeling in my stomach told me keeping Gabe was a huge, awful mistake. It reflected poorly on my character. Why didn't I just leave her there? Why didn't I kill her? What about this barely adult girl captivated me? I looked back down at her. Her face was sweaty and pale, her lips chapped and flaky.

I turned around, eager to leave her to her own thoughts and pains, but she grabbed for me, her fingers brushing against my leg. I caught the gaze of her deep blue eyes. I noted the sore, deep bruises from the ropes that had snaked around her wrists.

"We can't stay here. There are too many of them," she said. "There are hundreds. We need to leave soon."

"I know. Once you're feeling better we're going to pack up and find Frank."

"Frank? You're not still considering that, are you?"

My compassion for her vanished. "Yeah, I am. We can leave and look for him in the immediate area. If we can't find him, we'll come up with something else."

"I don't believe you. We're going to get killed looking."

"Listen. No one ever said we have to be a 'we.'" I sighed. "You can go your own way whenever you want. It's up to you. As long as you're with me, I'll try not to kill you and we'll see where things go," I bargained, knowing I was being stupid. I shouldn't have to plan around her. But maybe this was what consoling the sick was all about—letting your life revolve around someone else for a change.

* * *

Sitting by the sliding glass door, I watched the sea of undead in the streets below, undulating, growing rapidly. The horrendous weather continued on, the sky turning darker with the approaching night. Once it became too dark to make out the forms of corpses, I broke from my thoughtless daze and stood up.

With no warning, pressure and dizziness clouded my brain. My vision darkened and became fuzzy. I froze, bringing my hand to my head. It could have been a concussion. The blows dealt to my head by Gabe warranted head trauma, I was sure.

Noise from the hallway demanded my attention. I glanced to my left and saw the vague outline of Gabe leaning against the wall.

"Well? What's the plan?"

The light was strange. Her shadowy figure faded in and out of my vision. If I stared too long, I'd lose her, but if I didn't focus hard enough, I wouldn't be able to see her.

"I didn't think about it. I was just..." Sitting there? Staring at the faces of decomposing, once lively humans? Yeah, that was it.

Apparently she knew my answer without me delivering it. "We'll leave in the morning then."

I laughed at her command. "Where are we going to go?"

"I don't know. We'll go on an adventure—Robinson Crusoe style or something."

"Have you even read Robinson Crusoe?" My question silenced her. I hadn't read it until a few weeks ago. But it still made me better than her. No denying that.

"Listen, Cyrus, when I was hanging off a building going insane I came to a few life realizations. One, us sitting around in this apartment will result in death. Either yours or mine, but one of us will probably die, regardless of any half-assed promises. We just don't get along on a basic level." She was as high up on her soapbox as she could get. "Two, I feel like I have nothing to lose. The world as I know it has come to a complete and fucking end. It'll never be the same, so I might as well live it up while I'm still alive and in decent condition."

I scratched the side of my jaw in pensive consideration. It was clear enough she was ready to put our misunderstandings behind us and go the route of an insane loner, much like myself. Perhaps throwing that girl off a balcony was the best thing I could've done. Now I had a partner in crime. Hopefully our current breakdown of the situation would put her sporadic, bipolar past behind us.

I'm aware I seem like the kind of person who needs no one, which is correct. I don't. However, the idea of conditioning someone to be like me, a companion in the new world, wasn't a thought entirely unappealing. A part of me was aware Gabriella wouldn't put up with me terrorizing her forever, but another part sure hoped she would.

Whatever made that girl tick was going to keep on ticking until she ran out of batteries. After that, when would I find another woman? Mentally slapping myself for such a ridiculous train of thought, I shoved the ideas away and focused on Gabe's question.

"What's your definition of 'living it up?'"

"I'd like to light a candle first, since its pitch black in here," she said, "if that isn't too much to ask. I'm pretty sure all the zombies in Seattle know we're here. There's no point in hiding."

* * *

Twenty minutes later, three matches and a candle found, we were sitting in the living room, discussing a plan. Gabe had a bottle of water. I had my last bag of marshmallows. We were peachy keen, like kids at a campfire. I didn't understand why I spent so long looking for a candle when I had a battery operated halogen lamp. Guess it was for ambiance.

"You were right," Gabe said. "The apartment has held up well. Being here isn't just a matter of our safety, though. It's a matter of supplies."

A slightly stale marshmallow rolled around in my mouth as I nodded. I prodded it with my tongue until it was out of the way, pressing against my cheek. "That door is solid steel and bolted well. We can go that way, but I hear them out there all day and night. The best bet is to go to the roof via the balcony."

She nodded, the wheels in her mind turning. I already had a precise plan formed on exiting the apartment, but it amused me to let her 'think' about it. She seemed to like being part of arranging things, so I let her. It wouldn't hurt anyone.

The single candle flickered, throwing the shadows on her face into a dancing frenzy. She looked like a monster, but who was I to talk?

Laying on my stomach, I propped up my head in my hands. A little someone wiggled into the side of my t-shirt and cuddled up against my ribs. I pulled down the neckline of the shirt and looked at Pickle. The candle light barely made it through the white cotton, but it illuminated her tiny red eyes.

Gabe spoke, drawing my attention away from the adorable albino at my side. "What do we bring? I've never had the chance to pack useful things or take what I needed."

The ball was back in my court. I'd let her initiate our escape plans, but now it was time for me to take over again. "We'll pack up as much as we can without being excessive. Be practical, light, and efficient. No bringing a rocket launcher just for kicks."

Her brows furrowed. "Do you have one?"

I grinned and got up, sending Pickle scurrying out of my shirt and under the dining room table as I sauntered off into my spare room.

We got to packing. Regret pained my heart as I sorted through what was reasonable to take and what wasn't. The contents of that room were the closest thing to children that I'd ever have, and here I had to pick between them. It was a parent's worst nightmare.

At first I beat myself up about leaving the apartment, since there wasn't a concrete reason to do it. Gabe thought she convinced me, but in the end I convinced myself. Sure, I didn't need to leave, but I wanted to. Everyone needs a little danger to spice up their lives.

All of it struck me as funny in that moment. The teenage feminist and the sociopath, packing our bags before setting out for a day on the undead town. I didn't see a single issue with it, and Gabe didn't either, I hoped. Just because she was on board now, didn't mean she'd always be. But despite that...

The world was our oyster. Hell, the pearl inside of it was too, not that we needed it.

Chapter 6

I wasn't going to wait for Francis anymore.

The thought hit me when I stepped into the spare room. The realization felt like a door slamming in my face. But it had been, what, two weeks? Frank wouldn't want me to wait this long under the circumstances. He'd told me it took two hours to get from the cabin to Seattle. Two weeks seemed like too long. He was probably dead.

Pushing the thought away, I focused on what was important—supplies. After assessing the contents in the spare room I was disappointed in how I'd been rationing my MREs. We'd been eating two a day since she arrived, and before that I'd been eating two or three since they apocalypse started. If we started eating one each a day, we could stretch them out to last three months. After that, we'd slowly starve. Food was limited, the undead were abundant.

Zombies, I thought as I rationed out MREs. Who knew it would be zombies?

Through the walls of the spare room, I could hear the white noise of their groans. I got used to it, but every once in a while it was impossible to ignore. After a few moments of listening, I phased it out.

An entire wall was covered in guns, all mounted and shiny. My Barrett .50 mournfully stared at me from the center of this display. I wouldn't be taking that lover with me.

I caressed my P90, stroked my M14, admired my collection of side arms, especially the Desert Eagle. It had sentimental value. The G3 looked as sleek as ever. The M4 Carbine reminded me of my younger days. My two shotguns, W1200 and M1014, begged to be fired.

On the floor, a M249 SAW stood, casually left out from the last time I cleaned it. Too heavy to take, it would stay alone in my apartment forever.

The Barrett, though, I couldn't leave. Not with 10 shots waiting to be fired. 10 one-shot, one-kill bullets. I justified it necessary to bring it up to the roof to clear any hindrances. Then I could get just a couple shots off. That's all I wanted.

"I've seen these in videogames," Gabe said from beside me, gesturing towards the weapon. "That one especially. It's a Barrett."

"It is," I said, a little impressed, but unwilling to show it.

A smile tugged at the corner of her mouth as though she sensed how I felt. What was it with women and *knowing* things? On average, I could only identify two major emotions in people: anger and fear.

"So, what're we bringing?"

I looked at the two neat stacks of MREs and nothing else. "Food, water, ammunition, space blankets."

"Maybe some medical stuff? Rubbing alcohol, gauze. The monsters out there aren't the only ones who could hurt us."

I would've packed everything of necessity eventually, but my mind seemed a bit bogged down and hers didn't. I gave her credit for the quick thinking and let her start rifling around the room for items.

"This?" she'd ask.

"Mhm."

"And this?"

"Sure."

It was handy having her around, but I knew I couldn't get used to her. I started thinking about Frank again. I got used to him, and now had to suffer because of it. Gabe knew we were going to look for him when we left. There was no way I was going to give up without trying. Even if I found his remains up and walking, eager to eat me, at least I'd know his fate.

By the time we trimmed surplus items from our packs, it felt late and I was ready to go to sleep. I still took the time to set my Barrett, loaded, by the sliding glass door to take up to the roof when the time came. The rock climbing gear I regretted buying last year was by the gun. At the time I had no use for it, but now we were going to use it to safely rappel down the building. Having everything set up and ready to go gave me a small sense of reassurance.

Tiredness swept over me as I headed towards my room. That feeling tripled when Gabe came from the spare room, candle in hand, evidently wanting to talk.

"How long are we going to look for Frank? Where will we look?"

"I don't know." I sighed. "We'll search a two block perimeter. When we leave town, we'll probably find a sign of him on the roads."

I thought her questioning was through. It wasn't.

"If we don't find him, where will we go? We never talked about it."

Her comment roused me. Gabe and I talked about looking and waiting for Francis, but during those conversations we never talked about where we'd go if we couldn't find him. I couldn't go to his cabin; I didn't know where it was. I did know it was east, past the smaller towns up in the mountains. However, the exact location eluded me. Trying to get there was a joke, but planning to go east was a good idea.

The roads would be choked the closer we came to Seattle's limits. Other people would've tried to get out, but they would've panicked and left en masse. Since we'd be coming late to the game, we wouldn't have to compete with thousands of the living jockeying for road space. The highways were smaller the farther out you went. If we went by foot when required, it wouldn't be a problem.

"We'll just go east," I said. "I'm sure once we get out of the hot zones we'll figure the rest out."

Pickle brushed up against my leg. I hadn't seen her in quite a few hours, so her presence was comforting. I picked her up, letting her climb up onto my shoulder.

"I'm surprised you have a pet."

Oh, boy. She just couldn't shut up. I tried to show via body language I was done talking, but I wasn't sure how. I ended up looking restless as I glanced at my room.

Gabe took the hint and smiled halfheartedly before squeezing past me into the living room. I waited until I heard her settle into the sleeping bag I gave her before going into my own room. I shut the door and fell onto the bed.

I was done with talking. Done with planning. I just wanted to sleep.

Chapter 7

The weather got its act together and remembered what it should be doing. Sunlight broke through the morning mist, dissipating the grey clouds. I stared, entranced, at the small strip of sky just above the building next to mine. For a second I wished today would be normal. I'd work out, read my magazines and other relevant periodicals, then go work the night shift at the pharmacy. My daydream was brief, ending as I threw back the covers and made my bed for the last time. It seemed like the right thing to do, though irrational, and I took this quiet time to let my mind go blank.

After I ate an MRE (Cheese tortellini), I rationed a bottle of water for tooth brushing and a miniscule sponge bath, again taking my time. Rushing things now would create a bad start for the rest of the day, for the rest of however long it was going to take to get somewhere safe. As I readied myself, I listened for their sounds outside but heard none. The stiffs dissipated overnight from the lack of stimuli.

I got dressed. My barely used combat attire was stiff, as I hadn't worn it yet. Under my pocket-laden tactical vest I wore a black, Ripstop tactical shirt, with a pair of coordinating

Ripstop Tru-Spec pants to finish off the look. When browsing the internet for things like this, anything with the word 'tactical' seemed to work out just fine.

By the time I finished getting ready and packing ferret food, I expected Gabe to be waking up, but she was still sleeping on the living room floor. Everything was ready to go—everything but her. Cutting her beauty sleep short, I pushed her onto her back with my foot.

"Hey, get your act together. It's time to go."

She opened her eyes wide and scrambled to her feet, reaching for her shoes at the same time. "Sorry."

"I'm going to bring everything to the balcony and check out the situation. Eat something, drink some water, and meet me out there."

As I suspected, there weren't many undead outside. None of them even noticed me as I dragged our packs and everything else out. Since there were so few in the street, I doubted there were many more in the alley. I wasn't going to need the Barrett.

Gabe picked up the pace and was on the balcony just as I grew impatient. She looked up at the brick wall between us and the roof, then back to me.

"How are we getting up there?"

"You get on my shoulders and I'll boost you up. Take this rope and loop it around something so we can lift the supplies."

I explained how getting on my shoulders worked. Leaning forward, I braced my hands on my knees so she could place her right foot atop my right thigh. Her hands went to my shoulders for support. The physical contact made me uncomfortable, but I ignored the feeling for the sake of practicality.

Gabe worked her feet up to my shoulders and grabbed my offered hands so she could stand. She must've weighed around a hundred pounds, so the pressure of her feet on my shoulders was bearable.

When we were both standing straight, Gabe's forearms had just enough room to lay flat on the side of the ledge. This is where I got worried. It took a lot of strength to haul up one's own bodyweight. She didn't weigh much, but if she couldn't get a good burst of adrenaline, we'd have to figure out another way up there.

"Are you ready? You need to go. I can't stand here forever."

After a few seconds, I felt one foot lift off and heard it connect with the brick wall as she tried to gain leverage. It was now or never. The second I felt her other foot leave my shoulder, I grabbed the heels of her boots and pushed her upward. My effort paid off as I saw her disappear over the ledge.

Soon after, one end of the rope I gave her hit my face, followed by the sound of laughter. After rubbing my cheek, I looked up and saw Gabe grinning.

"Sorry," she said, but there was no regret.

Letting the shot with the rope go, I tied one end to a pack and lifted it above my head, reducing the distance she had to pull it up. We repeated the process until all items were on the roof.

"I'm going to get Pickle."

I saved her for last because I didn't want to cause my ferret panic. Pickle was trained to stay in small spaces without losing it. Days after I bought her, I began training her for situations like this. I was paranoid and didn't ever want to risk leaving her. For the ride to the roof, I left her in her travel cage. I brought her out, thankful for her silence, and tied the top handle to the rope. The trip was going to be hell for her, but I couldn't let her die.

Gabe was sensitive to my adoration for the ferret, and pulled the rope slowly and smoother than with the other gear. I felt appreciation and gratefulness towards her and didn't bother to suppress it.

Once I climbed the rope and stood on the roof, I took a look around. Dark smoke rose into the clouds from the direction of Puget Sound. I could barely see it between the tall buildings of downtown, but there was just enough space to catch it. That explained the lack of Zs. They were shuffling towards the latest excitement.

This is heavy, I thought as I shrugged my backpack on, Pickle now transferred inside it. *Did I pack too much?*

I put her in the outer zipper pocket of the pack, separated from the rest of my gear. Pickle settled in after much defiant wriggling. Gabe and I crossed the barren rooftop, keeping an eye on the roof access hatch. We leaned over the other edge to see the alley.

It was empty. Luck wasn't something I relied on, but it was helpful. She'd rappel down, since I could cover both ends of the alley with the Barrett, then I'd follow. From there we went on foot. I had a car in the underground garage across the street, but there was no way in hell we were going to go get it. The entrance was visible from the balcony, but was blocked by a red sports car and a minivan. We'd rough it out on foot until it was safe to hotwire a car.

After I secured the rope around a huge metal ventilation system, I helped her into the climbing harness and showed her how to control the belay device.

"Try to walk against the wall around the windows. We'll go unnoticed longer if the ones inside don't see you. Once we're down, keep the talking to a minimum."

Then she was off, rappelling down the building as though she'd done it a million times before. I wondered if she'd done any rock climbing back in the day, but it was too late to ask her. By the time I thought of it, she was halfway down. There was no point in using the Barrett to cover her. I waited until she retrieved the 9mm I gave her before I started down, too.

When I got to the bottom, she pointed to the two exits of the alley. Right or left? Did it matter? We didn't know what was on either end, but I chose right just for the hell of it. As we walked, I brought up my carbine, the main rifle I'd be using.

Single file, guns on the ready, we moved silently around dumpsters and garbage, each footstep taking us farther down the block and closer to the unknown.

I maneuvered around an indistinguishable pile of gore, opting to breathe through my mouth as we passed. Whatever it was, it was teeming with wiggling maggots. Though it was probably a trick of my mind, I could've sworn I actually heard them.

We came to the end of the alley and took in the chaotic intersection before us.

It wasn't uncommon to find narrow, cramped streets in Seattle, but the intersection managed to take the word 'cramped' to a new level. To the right, two Humvees were head to head, completely blocking traffic. The traffic lights were destroyed, creating a bridge between all the wrecked cars beyond the Humvees. Evidence of a fire was obvious. Crispy, burnt corpses fell half-way out of blackened, melted cars. Even from my angle, I could see the glimmering lake of glass surrounding the entire scene, both from broken cars and the surrounding shops.

To my left, the chaos was relatively serene. Only the businesses had been looted, and wreckage was sparse in the street. Somehow the government, city, or whoever the fuck tried, managed to block off the street. Farther up, I knew it turned onto the I-5 freeway, which was fortunate for us. It meant there was a clear path out of Seattle.

I made a left and moved down the sidewalk, careful not to walk close to open doorways. Some stores were still untouched, as though an apocalypse never happened. A boutique, one that I had passed before on my way to work, still boasted outrageously expensive purses and shoes. The mannequins looked down their noses at me, as grandiose and absurd as they always had.

Fuck you, Louis Vuitton, I thought spitefully. *No one's going to you now.*

Other shops weren't as fortunate. We crunched past one that must've gone through an outrageous fire. The entire inside was a macabre tangle of burnt furniture and countertops. Scorched corpses littered the ground. Maybe they had made a stand there. Or tried to, at least.

From down the street came the roar of a vehicle. Gabe and I froze, anticipating the certain moans of zombies to follow.

"This changes things," Gabe said.

I shook my head. "No, it doesn't. We're bound to run into people at one point or another. Maybe they'll want to give us a ride."

Maybe it's Frank. I kept that thought to myself.

A jet black Hummer swiveled around the corner, moving steadily down the street. They probably came from the freeway, which would confirm my suspicions. Confirmation of a cleared freeway would expedite our plans, whatever they were.

We were in plain sight, standing on the sidewalk. The Hummer was clearly making its way for us. I didn't bring my rifle up, figuring they'd feel threatened and run me over. A speeding vehicle headed for me was one thing I couldn't avoid. Zombies? No problem. Bipolar teenage girl? Whatever.

"Oh, shit," Gabe muttered.

"What is it?" I sighed.

"I know them."

"So? Shouldn't that make it easier to get a lift?"

She just shook her head.

Frankly, I didn't care about her issues, so I waited for the Hummer to pull up beside us, the tinted window rolling down. First thing I noticed: the man had too many greasy, flabby chins to count.

"Gabriella. Funny thing, running into you here," he said.

Her voice was flat, but I could tell she was shook up. "Yeah, Tyler. What the fuck are you doing here?"

"Lookin' for you," someone from the passenger side said.

"Listen, why don't we talk about this inside?" I ventured, pointing down the block to the zombies who had taken an interest in what was going on. Most of them were coming from the wreckage, trying to crawl over it all, but the rest were coming from the alley we'd just come from.

A crowd of zombies shambled toward us, and I wished I could enjoy it. They appeared to be remains of a football team, their colors black and orange. Some of the players even had helmets on, and I felt a tiny pang of sadness for them. How could they take a tasty, hot bite of living flesh if they had a big ol' helmet on? Poor zombies.

"Sure, sure," Tyler said. "Hop in the back, eh? Pull anything and we'll put a fuckin' bullet in your head."

He rolled up the window. We heard the automatic locks click. I looked at Gabe, raising an eyebrow. She said nothing as she yanked the door open, getting inside. I followed, settling into the leather seats.

The other man in the car was the comic opposite of Tyler. He was thin and sallow with a viciously hooked nose. Thinning brown hair was slicked back with natural hair gel.

"Gabby, nice to see you. Been looking for you for a while now," the skinny one said.

"Oh really? I'd thought you'd be worrying about other things, Larry."

I let my gaze roam around, zoning out from their conversation. Why listen to the hired help? You wouldn't listen to the ramblings of a taxi driver, would you? These clowns would be the equivalent if I got my way.

The back contained an absolute armory. Countless sub machine guns were piled on top of each other, but a few quality assault rifles and shotguns were at the party, too. These fuckers knew how to handle themselves. Or they were just good at hoarding expensive firearms.

With impassive interest, I looked away from the goods and up to Tyler and Larry, who were still carrying on with their dull conversation.

"...just left them like that. We came to get you, you—" Larry was rambling.

If I shot Tyler in the head...

"...so we's come to get you, right? Been chasing you since—"

No, can't shoot him first. The car was still on and wasn't in park. He could hit the gas and run us into a wall.

"You could imagine how hurt we all were..."

Hell, I have two handguns! I could hold them both hostage and kill them later. Using the rifle wasn't possible. It would be too awkward to yield in the amount of time needed. I wondered if I could even get the 9mm out fast enough.

"Hey! Ginger-boy, you payin' attention? We don't need no extra baggage. Get out of the car," Tyler shouted.

The Hummer had moved farther up the street. While I was zoning out, they evidently drove away from the Zs. Now, they wanted to offload me. I looked at Gabe and raised a brow.

Larry reached for a gun in a drink holder up front.

"Okay, okay," I said, getting the hint, and opened the door.

"Cyrus," Gabe started, but I shook my head.

"Don't worry about it. I got this. See you boys later."

While feigning getting out of the Hummer, my hand went for the knife strapped to my thigh, hidden from the two men. I swung back with lightning speed and flung myself onto Larry, ramming the knife in his throat. Arterial spray coated the windshield and my face, as I turned and grabbed Tyler's wrist. He was going for the handgun stashed in the drink holder. I twisted his hand, breaking it instantly. I realized I was in an awkward position—half my body in the backseat while I tried to take down the fat man in the driver's seat.

"What the fuck are you waiting for? Shoot him!" I yelled at Gabe as I fought with Tyler's other arm.

Blood from Larry spurted, getting into my eyes. Before too much of the salty liquid violated me, I squeezed my eyes and mouth shut. I heard the single shot, and another spray of blood, and this time gore, splashed into my face.

Dropping my hands from the lifeless body, I slid back into the seat next to Gabe.

"Really? What the fuck? You couldn't have shot him in the side of the head? How did you even get to that angle? You could've shot me."

Her bullet was a hollow point, effectively blowing up the front of poor old Tyler's noggin. I wiped the blood out of my eyes and reached over to shut the open door of the Hummer.

I looked at Gabe, who was white as a ghost.

"Well?" I demanded. "What the hell just happened?"

The front seat and passenger side were bloody. The windshield was bloody. I was bloody. Gabe was perfectly clean. I was getting angry.

Larry's body twitched. I grabbed Gabe's handgun and shot him in the head. A knife to the throat meant he was going to come back.

"I...I just...why did you do that? Why did you kill Larry?"

Uninterested in keeping up with her issues, I punched her in the temple. Hard. She slumped down, but was still conscious. Gabe was about to make another comment, but I punched her again, effectively rendering her unconscious.

Sweet silence. Some time to think and analyze the situation. A lot had just happened. Two ugly motherfuckers just tried to abduct Gabe and get rid of me. The distasteful and coppery scent of death filled the car. Gabe was unconscious. I was covered in gore.

Outside the situation hadn't grown any worse. No zombies. I jumped out of the car, opening the driver's side, and pulled Tyler out.

"Sorry, buddy," I muttered as I took his place.

Hunched over Larry, I opened his door, pushing him out. Now that problem was solved. After finding some fast food napkins in the glove compartment, I cleaned off the windshield as much as possible, concerned about the blood seeping into the ventilation system. Would that break it, or something? I know a lot of crap, but nothing about vehicles.

So I wouldn't crush Pickle, I shrugged my backpack off and set it in the front seat. I unzipped it, ready to let her come out on her own time. After watching the opening for a bit, I understood she was too scared to get out.

The car was still running, so I put it in drive and we went on our way. I felt icky and disgruntled, but it wasn't going to get in the way. I left my apartment, my haven, for a reason. Well, I wasn't sure what that reason was yet, but someday I'd figure it out.

As I drove, my conscience reared its ugly head. I didn't need to hit Gabe. Who was I turning into these days? I was more unstable than she was. Reaching back with one hand I grabbed her wrist, just to be sure I could feel a pulse. What was done was done, but I planned on apologizing when she woke up. I'm sure she'd feel better if I did.

But that didn't change the fact that I was one step away from losing it. The second I thought about a loss of control, Frank popped into my mind. I had to keep it together. Now I could start looking for him. If I didn't find him...

I *would* lose it.

Chapter 8

The freeway was emptier than I thought it would be. A few cars congested the entrances, but the Hummer nudged them aside easily.

I only drove a bit before realizing the error in my decision to hit the freeway so soon. There was no point in driving out, not finding Frank, and backtracking. Undead were making their way towards the general area of my apartment, enticed by the ruckus with Larry and Tyler. The longer I waited to return, the more there could be. I needed to rule out the area near my apartment before risking the freeway.

As I turned around, Pickle came out and sat in the passenger seat, catching a breather from the backpack and trauma to date. What a trooper.

Brain matter had dripped onto my face and into my mouth. The taste was not totally unlikable, but the thought that it had been from a fat weirdo was. You win some and you lose some.

After completing my turn, I parked the car (stopped it in the middle of the road), turned it off, and got into the backseat with Gabe. It was time to go back to the city and I needed her awake for it.

She was slumped against the seat, her chin touching her chest. She'd have one hell of a neck ache when she woke up. Probably a headache, too.

I lightly tapped her cheek a few times in attempts to rouse her. Nothing. I tapped a little harder. Her eyes fluttered open and she groaned.

"Fuck, Cyrus. Why'd you have to hit me?"

"Didn't feel like putting up with your girly whining. There was man's work to be done."

She rolled her neck, which emitted a series of cracks and pops, then rubbed her temples. "Man's work?"

"Man's work. And, Gabe?"

"Yeah?"

"I'm sorry for hitting you."

Gabe stared at me, brow furrowed in pain. She opened her mouth then closed it—rubbed her temples. Pickle scurried up the passenger's seat and perched on the headrest, looking at us.

"Okay, well, what now?"

"You know what we're doing. We're looking for him."

"Right. How could I forget?"

I didn't think about where to look. Once we were near my apartment all I did was drive down clear roads and backtrack until I found another. We drove like that for a while, each road revealing nothing but wreckage and the occasional stiff. My efforts were yielding no results, and I had no problem admitting it. It seemed unlikely I'd just happen upon Frank walking around. There was one thing I wanted to try before abandoning the cause completely.

"We're going back to my apartment. He might've headed that way after hearing gunshots. If he isn't there, we'll leave the city. I promise."

"Okay. It's not like I have a choice," she said, pushing past me to sit in the front seat. Pickle squeaked and ran off under the backseats.

I won all my battles. Cyrus V. Sinclair. The V stood for victorious. Every time.

* * *

On the way back to my place, we (mostly I) devised a plan. Gabe would park and hang low while I got back into the apartment and searched the area. I knew I could get up the rope with enough effort, and once I did I'd check the apartment, hallway, and just down the stairs. I doubted he'd be anywhere else.

"So, who were those guys?" I asked casually as we drove along, running over the occasional zombie road-blocker. Their bodies thumped beneath the tires, while others hit the hood, leaving slimy residue behind. Nothing the windshield wipers couldn't fix.

"Some people I used to work with."

"Why were they after you?"

She exhaled dramatically. "Weren't you listening? My boss seems to have gone crazy and sent his two dogs to retrieve me."

Gabe's voice was shaky when she answered, her eyes too big. Lies were easy to detect if you were paying attention. She knew I hadn't been paying attention, but why was she lying to begin with?

I whistled low. "That sounds pretty crazy. In the middle of an apocalypse, some manager sent some dudes to get you?"

"It's complicated. You wouldn't understand."

"Try me."

"Well, he's kind of in a gang. Real hardcore. Killin' people, running drugs, whole nine yards. In a time of need, I started working for him. Accidentally knocked off a few of his people when they couldn't keep to themselves. So that pissed them off quite a bit. After taking a lot of shit the scene threw at me, I told some secrets to some competitors of his then hit the road. I went across the entire country and he still found me. Great luck, huh?"

A little girl in a gang, killing people? I could believe the gang part. Seattle was getting a lot of attention for gang-related violence before the apocalypse happened. What seemed unrealistic was "knocking off" her leaders' people. Just because the world was undergoing some difficult changes, and she had been through some gnarly stuff, didn't mean she could feed me a lie like that and expect me to swallow it. However, in a way, it did make sense. Her ability to use a weapon wasn't too bad, and since she had survived as long as she had, well, I suppose it was possible she could've been involved with gangs. It would've taught her how to be a cutthroat.

Why am I even entertaining the idea of her having ties to a gang?

"What did you do for him, exactly?"

She made a face then rolled her eyes. "What do you think I did? How do you think I learned how to use a gun? They used me to get to people. Kill them."

I laughed. "Hit woman."

She glared. Little Gabriella, hit woman.

"Why would he have you knock off people?" Then, in an attempt to provoke her, "Why not put you in another position, if you catch my drift."

"Fuck you, Cyrus. Just because I'm pretty doesn't mean I have to be a whore!"

"Who said you were pretty?"

I breathed in the coppery scent of blood wafting around the Hummer, and made a note to clean it up a bit. Material objects needed to be maintained in order to function, and losing the mobile fortress would be terrible.

My fingers felt icy cold on the steering wheel. I turned the heater on, marveling at the blood that managed to penetrate every crevice of the console. As the heat pushed out of vents, it created ripples in the red liquid.

We drove in silence until we were a block away from the apartment. I turned the Hummer off, scanning the area. There were no zombies in sight. For an undead apocalypse in a city of thousands, there wasn't much of a challenge around.

Pickle climbed up the back of my seat, then on to my shoulder. I stroked her fur as I considered what route I'd take back to my place.

I peeled the albino ferret off and placed her on the dashboard, then moved into the backseat, checking out what goods I could take on my mission. After surveying the situation, I decided to leave my carbine behind and opt for something that offered more mobility. Not wanting to be bogged down, I left my pack and took my 9mm. Before I opened the car door, I snatched a radio from the backpack and threw it at Gabe.

Sitting on the backseat, preparing to leave, I stared at Pickle licking blood off the dash. To my right, Gabe stared out the front window, radio in hand.

"I'd consider laying down back here, or something, so the Zs don't see you," I said as I slid the clip out then pushed it back in. I pulled the hammer back, checking to make sure there was a bullet in the chamber.

"It's not like they couldn't get in if there were enough of them."

"Probably couldn't, actually. This glass is likely bullet proof. I don't think your pimp messes around."

"Listen, you fuc—"

Before she could say anymore, I was out of the car, jogging down the street. It felt good to be truly alone again. No morally confused woman by my side.

Chapter 9

The empty apartment was just as I had left it. Candy wrappers still on the dining room table, a candle on the living room floor. How easy would it be to just stay there? Gabe now had an arsenal in her possession, and a loaded Hummer. It's not like I'd be leaving her to die. I could wait for Frank without anyone telling me to do otherwise.

Then I remembered Pickle, alone in that gore stained vehicle with a lunatic. So much for staying.

Francis wasn't in the alleyway or on the roof. There were no signs of him in my apartment either, but I knew I had to check the hallway too. Unlocking the door took longer than I expected, but I wasn't on a time restraint. The hallway was empty. The thudding in Apartment 8 continued.

Sticking to the middle of the hallway, I walked down the stairs until I saw a figure in the lobby, but it wasn't Francis. It's thin, still body gave it away. The undead were often statuesque when unprovoked by the living. After quietly going back to my apartment and locking up, I was sure Frank hadn't been there.

Unwilling to write the trip off as a complete disaster, I grabbed a duffle bag from the spare room and filled it with a few remaining MREs and some ammunition we couldn't carry the first round. It only took a few minutes, but it was worth it. I dragged it outside and tied one end of the hanging rope to it before climbing up. After pulling the bag up, I carried it across the roof. Panting from the effort of searching and packing, I took a deep breath before taking out the radio.

"You alive?"

"Yeah, I'm here. The coast is still clear, captain." Gabe was belligerent as usual.

"Okay, come get me."

"Hold on. I think I see—"

The radio went silent, and I stared at the device. Had I lost Gabe already? Did someone come out of nowhere and hijack both her and the Hummer? I leaned over the roof and cast a long look up and down the alley, finding nothing.

A few moments later, the rumbling of an engine came closer.

"I have someone with me. Pretty sure it's your buddy Frank," Gabe said. "I'm on my way. Start lowering. The sunroof is open."

I had the bag half way down the building when the black Hummer made its appearance. At first nothing followed it, but a handful of zombies made their dull, inevitable approach.

My hands were busy lowering, so I couldn't scold Gabe for being less than careful. As I worked, I started feeling overwhelmed Frank found *us*. I hadn't given up, but I'd become so doubtful it was hard to believe it was him. But it couldn't be anyone else. It had to be Frank.

Tires screeching, the vehicle came to a stop. The same tactical-gear-clad girl I had met a few days ago poked up through the sunroof, looking back up at me. A second later, Francis popped up out of the sunroof, too.

"Stop jerkin' off, Cyrus! Get down here!"

Excitement gripped me and the rope loosened in my hands, sending the bag speeding to the vehicle. Just in time, I squeezed, stopping it before it hit the roof. The severe jerk strained my arms, forcing me to brace myself. There went my back.

Gabe and Francis grabbed the duffel, maneuvering it into the backseat. She got one of the rifles out and tried to pick off Zs that were getting too close. The noise would only draw more, but it was too risky to not take action.

I rappelled down, noting that all undead in the immediate area caught wind of the action and were ready to give chase. Both ends of the alley were choked with dead bodies, happily trotting along.

My boots touched the roof of the car. Francis was at the wheel, Gabe still shooting. She cleanly blew the head off a naked woman missing an arm.

"What's the plan, Cyrus? Reverse or forward?"

"Forward!" I told Frank. "Get some momentum so you can run them over."

"You got it, boy!"

I ducked into the vehicle, yanking Gabriella down with me.

"They're going to fly over the Hummer," I said. Just to keep her guessing, I lied and added, "Don't want you going with 'em."

G-force knocked me back a little when Frank put the pedal to the metal. Bodies hit the front of the car, thumping and soaring over the roof. They were no match for the stolen Hummer.

There were barricades set up back when the military was still trying, which left some roads wide open and others beyond the description of 'traffic.' Frank seemed to have a plan, so I didn't bother questioning him, although I wasn't sure why we didn't get on the freeway.

I glanced into the rearview mirror and noted the growing horde following us. A zombie wearing Mickey Mouse ears was in the lead.

"So, Cyrus. I'm surprised to see you outsid'a that hole you call a home. Did this firecracker ball-n-chain you, or what?"

If he were anyone else, I would've knocked him out for a comment like that. But he was Francis Bordeaux. He was the father I'd wished I had. The role model who came in too late. I remembered the regret from our last conversation, and decided

I'd never end a conversation with him negatively again. So, instead of being snide, I laughed with him and clapped him on the shoulder.

Gabe ejected her clip, checking to see how many rounds she had left. After slamming it back in, she looked at me skeptically, then up to Frank, who was still laughing at his 'ball-n-chain' remark.

"So this is Frank? He was walking around with a knapsack and a shotgun like it was nobody's business."

"Yeah, that's Frank. Nothing he does is anybody's business." I grinned.

Frank howled in the front seat as he hit a faceless teenager, who flew over the car and into a street light.

"So, what's the plan, ya'll? We gonna bunker down in the mountains? Head to the cabin?"

Gabe avoided eye contact. Frank's presence seemed to have stunned her. She didn't think we'd find him, and now that we had it probably felt like us against her. If she *was* thinking that, she was partially right. I had more control over our plans than her, but I was ready to let Frank call the shots for a while.

"There's going to be a ton of them the farther east we go," Gabe said. She was trying to be assertive. "I'm sure your cabin is overrun by now."

"Only one road that leads to my place. Then it's a full day's hike to the cabin. We just have to skirt around a couple towns and we're clear."

"What about food? Water?" Gabe continued seeking flaws in his plan. "What if we get there and run out of resources in a few weeks?"

My thoughts went back to his home in the Ozarks. Two words: self sustaining.

He merely chuckled.

"I don't think that's an answer," she prodded.

Scowling, I looked back at her. "If Frank thinks the cabin is a good idea, it is. Stop your bitching."

Maybe it was something in my voice, because she stopped her bitching.

Chapter 10

It had been a long time since I'd driven out of Seattle, and it was a while before I remembered the road system. Even though I had a car, I couldn't remember the last time I actually drove it. A few memories of driving to army surplus stores came into focus, along with driving to the local docks for gun pickups. Nothing out of the ordinary for good ol' Cyrus V. Sinclair. With the help of some interstate signs, my memory came back.

We managed to drive another twenty minutes on I-5 North before the roads became heavily congested. Cars ranged from bumper to bumper to impassible wreckage, which forced us to use surface streets. We made it on to SR 522 East. After three hours, we arrived at our first stop, a small town called Monroe. I projected the trip would normally taken 45 minutes tops, sans apocalypse.

The Hummer was low on gas by the time we reached the town. Roads were clear, and we glided down the off ramp into Monroe. It was late in the afternoon, but the sun was still warm and the visibility good. So far, we couldn't see any zombies, so we took a risk and decided to fill up the tank.

Frank maneuvered to a gas station without hitting too many cars. More noise, more zombies. The logic was flawless. Frank took the pump, while Gabe and I stood guard duty.

"The pump is electric," Gabe whispered to me. "How is he going to..."

"He's going to siphon it. Just keep your mouth shut, don't shoot unless you have to, and watch."

A fat kid with huge headphones shambled out of the convenience store next to the gas pumps. His cheeks were gnawed off. It was unbelievable he still had the headphones. I wondered how long he could walk around 'listening' to music until his player ran out of juice. Not really caring, I shot him. Other than him, the coast was clear.

And, sure enough, we heard gas gurgling.

"Hey, ya'll. We should consider getting something to put more gas in for the road. No telling when we're gonna get another lucky chance with a gas station."

"There's probably something in the store we can use. Gabe, you stay at the entrance. Frank and I'll go in. That okay with you?"

Frank nodded. Once the tank was full, we approached the building. The front of the store was dimly lit from the windows, but the back was pretty dark. I glanced at Frank and noticed he had no gun or flashlight.

He caught me looking and raised a machete at his side. "In 'Nam we didn't have flashlights, and when we ran out of bullets..." He shrugged.

My ears rang from the silence. The scent was surprisingly mild in the store. Back in Seattle, the scent of multiple rots was everywhere. You'd expect a gas station to be no exception. All it smelled like was stale pretzels and old pizza. The refrigerated section wasn't bad at all. Metal shelves were only mildly disheveled. No one had come in and raped the place like they did back home. Interesting.

We searched the small auto section and found no gas canisters or anything else of use. The only option would be to empty out pop liters and fill them back up. As Frank and I poured the fizzy drinks to the floor, I noticed the back room.

"There's probably something back there. Industrial containers, maybe. I'll go take a look."

Frank nodded, watching red soda pour onto the floor. I didn't need to wonder what he was thinking about.

Gun back out, I pressed the door open an inch and listened. No noise. No light, either. Bringing a flashlight out from my side holster, I let it roam across the room. Sure enough, there were large, lidded buckets stacked up against the wall. I confidently strode into the room, lowering my gun.

The lights turned back on.

I spun around, spots in my eyes from the harsh fluorescents. A greasy, rotten man with a beard waited for me.

He caught me off guard, knocking me onto the floor when he lunged. I fell back and landed in the buckets, loudly scattering them. Stagnant mop water sloshed out.

Greasy Beard didn't have a left hand, but he still had a mouth and a right hand, which was hazard enough for me. I tried fending him off with one arm while I grabbed for my 9mm. He dropped to his knees and moved toward me. The gun rested in the mop water, too far away for me to reach.

Putrid breath engulfed my face as the zombie groaned, his jaws snapping. His stump of a left hand streaked old, dark blood on my neck as he grabbed for me.

The 9mm wasn't a possibility. There was no way I could get to it and hold Greasy Beard off at the same time. I reached for my other gun, the .40, but it was on my other leg which was blocked by the Z. With a surge of strength, I heaved and pushed him off, sending him landing on his rump a few feet away.

I grabbed for my gun, turning around and—

There was a machete in the top of his skull. His mouth slowed down then stopped.

Frank put his foot against Greasy Beard's back and pushed, sending the zombie sprawling. Old blood escaped the head wound. Frank proceeded to wipe the machete on the back of the Zs jacket before letting it rest at his side.

"Well, now. That was kind of sloppy, wasn't it? You should've known to check everywhere before entering."

I grunted and kicked the truly dead undead on the floor before collecting as many buckets as I could carry.

"What's with these lights?" I asked. "Did you find a generator or something?"

The rest of the gas station was lit, pop machines and lotto ticket vending machines ablaze. Somewhere, speakers played static from an abandoned radio station.

"No, sir. Them lights just turned on by themselves,' Frank replied.

Outside was normal looking, except for a smoldering car in the intersection across the street and some dead bodies. Gabe leaned against the Hummer, looking up at the lit pumps.

Though the power was on in our location, it was hard to tell if it was on anywhere else.

"Rolling power," Gabe said as we filled the buckets with gasoline. "Sometimes power supplies go into an auto-conserve mode if there are errors in the system. It probably powers different sectors of the town every couple of hours or so."

If that were true, it explained the freshness of the gas station goodies. Power in Monroe also implied something dangerous. People would be considerably more willing to stay in the town if their modern comforts were still available, which meant Monroe was probably overflowing with people.

I voiced my thoughts to Gabe and Frank. Gabe seemed excited by the idea, Frank wary.

"What's the problem?" she protested. "More people means help, supplies, and shelter!"

"How long has it been since this thing started, girly?" Frank said slowly, acting as though she were daft (which in my opinion, she was).

"Maybe close to three months. It started in April, so it's about July now."

"You ever heard of people living in the woods all by themselves? How crazy they get 'cause they're in survival mode?"

I finished Frank's point. "In a situation like this, people will either become territorial animals or 'save-everyone' do-gooders."

"Like you said—there are do-gooders, Cyrus." She hopped into the car, slamming the door shut behind her.

Frank threw a pained, *what were you thinking?* look at me. "How have you handled that?"

"I don't know. I just do."

* * *

After consulting the map in the glove compartment, we decided to take a back road through Monroe. It was less likely to be congested and populated. There were straggling zombies here and there, but we either grazed or ran over the ones who got in the way.

We drove under an overpass and were feeling moderately confident when everything started to go downhill again. That's because we hit a roadblock of two police cars obstructing a roundabout. We had to get through if we wanted to continue on our merry way. Stuff couldn't work out forever, I guessed.

Frank and I left the Hummer with Gabe at the wheel. It was then I noticed a score of zombies about a block back. By the time we broke into one of the cop cars, put it in neutral, and rolled it away, the Zs would be on us.

I was about to use the butt of my gun to smash through the window of the cop car when Francis grabbed my shoulder.

"Don't go the hard way if there's an easy way right in front of you."

He proceeded to open the car door, grinning wisely.

We were rolling the car up onto a curb and into a small patch of grass when we heard a shout from the Hummer.

"Get the fu—"

I cranked the E-brake up on the car and peered over its hood. Some guy was at the wheel of the Hummer, driving straight at us through our cleared path. Gabe was nowhere in sight, but I guessed she was knocked out in the vehicle.

The gore-covered Hummer soared past us, a husky, bearded man glaring at us as he went by. My lips curled back in an angry snarl, and I reached toward my thigh holster as Frank set his hand on my shoulder.

"What's wrong, Cyrus? We can just start over. I got my pack and you got whatever's on ya. What else do some fellows need? Besides, didn't look like you were screwing that girl."

"That Hummer has my ferret in it."

His face went somber and he nodded in understanding.

Back in 99, Francis had given me a valuable piece of information. "You think you can rough it on your own, but you can't. You gotta love something and hold onto it. It'll keep you sane, even if you don't wanna be."

The lesson was that even if you think you're a badass, keeping something close to you to take care of keeps you mentally fit and sound. I was still working on the concept. Bottom line was Pickle was in that fucking Hummer, and I was going to get her back.

Luck was a rollercoaster. Only seconds before we were royally screwed, and the next it improved. The Hummer spun a hard right up a slight incline not too far away from us. I couldn't quite see over the few hills the road disappeared between, but I saw the tops of two towers. A large wooden sign the Hummer passed by confirmed my suspicions as to what the building was. Carved block letters read, "Monroe Reformatory." "Survivors" and a ^ were spray painted between the two words, a declaration that the prison had been taken over by crazies. The engine of the Hummer faded from earshot, leaving Frank and I alone.

The good news was we knew where the Hummer was headed. The bad news was "Survivors" implied multiple.

I glanced down the roundabout at the undead milling towards us. Nothing could be easy, could it? It was unreasonable how many zombies were around these days.

"Let's get a move on. This is going to take the rest of the day, I'd imagine."

"You lead the way," Frank said.

I thought about how I'd infiltrate. It was reasonable to estimate a minimum population of ten, and perhaps a maximum of thirty. I wasn't a god, and wouldn't be able to kill that many on short notice with no planning. If I did make it through to the Hummer and Pickle was in it, what would I do about Gabe? Should I go find her?

Putting my thoughts on hold, I formed a plan. Step one was to find the Hummer, with a sub-step of finding the keys if they weren't in there. Despite all the movies I'd seen, I was never motivated to learn how to hot wire a car. I was regretting it, but as they say; shoulda, woulda, coulda. But if I got far enough to find the keys, I'd consider saving Gabe. After explaining the overall scheme to Frank, we headed towards the prison.

The reformatory wasn't anything special—tall walls, fences, towers. It seemed like a good idea to tide over in there while the undead were running the earth. However, scavenging would be difficult, and if a single zombie got in there, their good idea would turn bad in a jiffy.

Luckily, Frank located the Hummer on the west side of the grounds within minutes of checking the perimeter. We were spotted by a woman who was missing most of her chest cavity, but I took care of that without any problems.

It was still light out, but twilight would soon be on its way. The sky grew warmer with the shades of a sunset, and the night promised to be clear. Good weather for a car re-hijacking. I fished my silencer out, twisted it onto the 9mm, and made my way to the fence.

I wanted things to remain as quiet as possible for as long as possible. Frank hadn't spoken more than a few words since we broke in. We both knew the moment we were discovered our mission would get a lot harder. Always prepared, I took a pair of wire cutters from my vest pocket and set to work. Items like that were necessities—you didn't have to use them solely on wire.

I worked until I had room enough to squeeze through. After bending the fence open as much as I could, we shimmied in. Despite our best effort the metal still rattled, and I winced at the sound. It wasn't too loud, but if anyone were listening...well, we'd be screwed.

Inside, the grounds were wide open and forgiving. Everywhere was either brown dead grass or the gray stone of buildings. Guard towers were vacant, as were the windows overlooking the fields of open space. Was everyone inside? The fences were all closed, so maybe they thought there was no threat?

Too bad for them, there was a threat. Me and Frank.

Still on my guard but more confident, I walked back to where we spotted my Hummer. It was a welcoming sight, still full of ammo, supplies, and keys. Whatever the hijacker wanted to do, it had prevented him from casing the vehicle. Inside was just as I left it, with two small alterations.

One, Gabe wasn't in it. Two, neither was Pickle.

I looked up into the lighted windows of the prison and frowned. Nothing could ever be easy, could it? I searched the vehicle a second time, but the results didn't change.

"There ain't no gain without some pain," Frank said. He walked towards the prison, unfazed by our misfortune.

Disgruntled, I jogged to catch up to him as he made it to the back of the prison to an unloading area I had seen earlier.

There were two docks, both with additional door entrances. Parked at the farthest dock was a cherry red Mustang, looking misplaced in the back of a prison. We went to the first door and stepped inside the Monroe "Survivors'" Reformatory.

Chapter 11

After opening the door, we were assaulted by a flood of cheering coming from somewhere within the building. I could make out a dimly lit, sweltering hallway. From the stone walls and the summer heat outside, the place must have been an oven around the clock.

There were no other doors in the hallway, so we had but one choice: forward. At the end of the hall, we found a metal staircase that went up and another corridor that led to the left. The cheering was coming from down this corridor, so I went up instead, ahead of Frank. (If I were holding a ferret and a bitchy girl hostage, I'd keep them as far away as possible from the general festivities.)

Upstairs were administrative offices, but the end of the hallway opened into a larger area. A roaring was coming from there, too, but the acoustics downstairs didn't carry it as far up here. Curious and taking advantage of my position, I inched over and looked down. After deciding we were safe, I motioned Frank over.

Below were cells, tiers of them, with huge open space in the middle. There were at least a hundred men, shouting and chanting. They had constructed some kind of podium in the middle of the lowest floor, and a priest, black robes and all, held his hands up for silence. Most of the congregation had some form of weapon slung on their back, as they looked up with reverence at the priest.

The cells were filled with women, some just kids. Something in me said I should be disturbed by what I saw. These women were going to be forcibly impregnated, then forced to give birth to babies who would undoubtedly be really, really screwed up. I grimaced at the ever-rising conscience within me. Why did it decide to show up during situations where I couldn't do anything?

It didn't take long for the heat to get to me. Outside the weather was balmy, but inside was humid and uncomfortable. Everything I was witnessing intensified my uneasiness. I wiped the back of my hand against my sweaty forehead and itched to unzip my tactical vest.

"Fellow survivors!" the priest bellowed. The room quieted. "We have gathered enough of them for the Great Beginning! There will be one for each of you, but only the strongest will take multiple."

My suspicions were confirmed.

"We will reproduce and create a new civilization. A greater one, immune to these demons."

I had to cover my mouth to prevent the building laughter from escaping. I thought about how Gabe would take to being one of their wives.

Oh. They didn't want the Hummer. They wanted Gabe.

"Well, I'll be damned. I didn't think they'd resort to this so soon," Frank whispered.

While it made sense a huge number of people would go berserk when a traumatic event—such as the dead rising—occurred, why in the fuck did people have to do things like this?

After the speech carried on another ten minutes, the group dispersed into the lower levels of the prison. Silence seeped into the building. I picked up on distant crying from the cells. Frank and I shared a look before continuing.

My back pressed against the walls, so I wasn't close to the railing where I could be seen, I hurried with Frank down the left wing. The closer we got, the louder the wails grew.

"Down here!"

Gabe stood in front of the bars. From her nose to chin, blood was thick and caked on. Knowing her, she probably put up a good fight before being imprisoned. Around her were a handful of women, crammed into the bunks and sitting far away. They glared when she shouted, hissing for her to be quiet.

Raising my finger to my lips, I hushed her, too. No crazies were visible, but that didn't mean they were out of earshot. Carefully, we made our way down a level to the cells. Not a soul stopped us. This was too easy.

The women all hushed when they saw us, cowering away into the back of their cells. This wasn't an uncommon occurrence for me, so I didn't take offense.

"I can't believe you're here," Gabe whispered once I was close enough.

"Yeah. Neither can I."

"Why did you come back?"

"The Hummer is an asset I don't want to lose. And my ferret was in it."

She glared at me. I grinned at her.

I set down my gun, studying the lock. It was operated electrically, probably from a control room somewhere nearby. The men had improvised, throwing a good ol' chain and padlock on the sliding part of the cell door, linking it to the stationary. During the sporadic bouts of electricity, they must've disabled the locks so they could use a more manual, primitive method.

"Who has the key to this?"

Gabe shrugged. "They knocked me out before I was put in here. I don't know."

From an adjacent cell, a middle-aged woman, skin midnight black and glistening with sweat, called out, "Jim-Jones-wannabe has the key to everything. He doesn't delegate, so no one else has a key."

I like her style, I thought. Straight to the point.

I went to her cell. "Do you know anything else?"

With arms more powerful than I could predict, she reached through and slammed me up against the bars. My teeth jammed up into my lower lip. I tasted blood.

"Listen, boy. I'm not interested in getting knocked up with a lunatic's baby. I'm not interested in letting it happen to the last of my daughters either."

Frank took his time stepping in to pry the woman's hands off me.

I rubbed my mouth and glared at her. "Was that really necessary?"

"Violence is the only way to get what you want," she said, moving on as though she hadn't hurt me. "Their leader comes by here alone first, to take his pick of us. Their meeting just ended, so you have about half hour tops before he comes rolling along. You kill him and unlock my cell."

I bared my bloody teeth at her in defiance. "Why the fuck would I do that for you?"

"I know where they keep their guns. We need them to take this place back," she said. "Plus, I know you're looking for your pet and I know where it is. When you come back, I'll tell you, but one of you needs to escort us to the guns."

As soon as she mentioned my albino companion, I nodded. She hit a sensitive spot. The idea of more weapons was appealing, too. She let me go and I took a few steps back, composing myself. It wasn't often that I was completely overpowered by a woman.

I surveyed the area, looking for a good spot to hide.

"He comes from this direction, usually," a woman offered, reaching her hand out from the bars to my right.

There was absolutely nowhere that provided cover, no matter what direction the guy came from. We would have to go up or down a flight of stairs to have a chance.

"Where does he take you?"

The black woman jerked her head back the direction I came from. "You came through the administration offices connected to the back entrance, I assume. He takes us to the warden's office. You can wait there."

"What do you think about this?" I asked Frank.

He shrugged. "You need to get Pickle. We need to get Gabe. Plus, we aren't going to just leave these ladies here."

If I had come alone, there wouldn't be a moral dilemma in leaving the women. But if it meant finding my ferret, I'd get that cell door open for them.

"Fine. We'll do it, but first tell me why I can trust you. How do you know all this?"

Jaw set, she said, "Because, honey, I was the warden."

* * *

A couple minutes later I was crouched under a desk, my 9mm sidearm out and silenced. This was going to be a stealth operation, one hundred percent, until I was driving that Hummer out. I waited for the target to arrive.

Frank was wedged between two large filing cabinets, his back pressed against the wall. The metal cabinets provided enough coverage he wouldn't be seen from the door.

Look at me, on a whacky adventure to save a woman I didn't know or care about. My life was looking more like a morbid sitcom by the minute. Regardless of my mental resistance to grouping up with people, or rescuing anyone, I was doing it a lot lately.

"You're a chosen one," I heard in the distance, waking me up from my musings.

"Fuck you, you cocksucking lunatic!"

"You will produce blessed children."

Yeah, it was definitely the crazy boss and his selection of the night. They came in and the door slammed. From my vantage point, I saw her scuffed boots and the hem of his robe. He shoved the woman to the ground, and she landed right in front of the desk. The only thing I saw in her eyes was anger. She didn't say a word or even acknowledge me before she pushed herself off the ground.

The meaty sound of a punch. The man stumbled and shouted, but I didn't watch from under the desk anymore. As I was rising up, the woman landed another hit to his side before he used his bodyweight to hurtle her against the desk.

He muttered about religious courage before he noticed one Cyrus V. Sinclair in front of him, gun pointed at his balding, fat head. The priest managed to sound out the letter "W" before my bullet entered between his eyes and remained in his brain. The woman shoved him off and straightened.

"What a hero."

Cyrus V. Sinclair. The V stands for valor, I guess. But her tone told me she wasn't grateful. She seemed passively upset that I took him out first. I gave her a curt nod.

Seconds after the crazy fell, Frank came from his hiding spot and began searching the body. He looked up at the woman, who was rubbing her knuckles. "What's your name, girlie?"

"Blaze Wright, ex-Marine."

With wild black hair and an angry scar down her right cheek, Blaze was quite the sight. Something about her seemed different and almost appealing to me. I scorned myself for checking her out.

I joined Frank in the search. A wooden cross was attached to a thin piece of twine, but no key was in sight. I ripped it off anyway, letting the cross slide from the twine and fall onto the ground. A key fell to the wood floor. It had been hiding behind the cross.There was one key, which meant all the padlocks were the same. That was luck if I ever saw it.

Frank found a a pistol with full rounds, but nothing else. He stood up and handed the woman the gun, safety off.

"Frank Bordeaux, 'Nam veteran. This here is Cyrus Sinclair."

The formalities were killing me.

"Great," she said. "Let's go."

We left without any more dialogue, making our way back down the office hallway to the stairs. When we arrived at the entrance to the cells, we heard a pained shout.

I broke into a run, taking stairs two at a time to get back to the cells. I almost tripped over a bloodied body when I got there. The man was unconscious, his face a pulpy mess.

The warden stood behind blood coated bars. It didn't take long to make the connection. She lured him in front of the cell and grabbed him, as she had with me. After that, his face got friendly with the bars.

Stepping around the body, I unlocked the cell. The warden came out, two women following. "Which one of you is coming with us?"

"I'll go," Frank said.

"Where's my ferret?" I interrupted.

With dark, angry eyes shifting to me, the warden told me where I could find Pickle.

"You're kidding."

"No, they keep all animals downstairs in the kitchen for eating. They probably haven't eaten that rodent yet because they still got bigger game. Blaze, can you come with us?"

Blaze didn't look happy, but she nodded and stepped beside Frank.

After telling the women to stay put, the warden gave me directions to the kitchen before she headed in the opposite direction towards the offices. Frank and Blaze took the lead. Before we separated, Frank gave Gabe his second revolver.

"Well, thanks for the heartfelt rescue," Gabe said as we jogged towards the kitchen.

Uninterested in a conversation, I ignored her and picked up the pace. We still had the advantage of stealth.

I didn't have time to keep feeling lucky. Two men with .22 rifles came out of a room down the hallway. Our presence took them by surprise, and I managed to shoot both in the chest before they got one shot off.

As I was walking away, two shots sounded off behind me. I jumped as I turned and saw Gabe walking away from the bodies. There were bullet holes in their heads.

"Why are you wasting ammo? They weren't coming back anytime soon!"

"They'd come back as runners. Blaze was talking about it in the cells. We don't have time to sit around."

I wasn't sure what she was carrying on about, but runners was a self-explanatory term. As we picked up the pace, I remembered a group of people running through zombies, but the zombies weren't turning to grab them. Were those runners? How the hell was that even possible? They were very bloody— one of them had been missing most of his thigh. That was in the beginning of the apocalypse. I hadn't noticed runners then because *everyone* was running. I'd probably seen my share of them, but hadn't been paying attention. I had a feeling I'd be seeing another soon enough. Being surrounded by living people who had to be killed made that inexorable.

As we barreled around a corner, I ran straight into a man holding a bayonet. A fucking authentic bayonet. My reaction time wasn't fast enough, and the knife cleanly slid into the outer meat of my shoulder. I gasped and pulled back, the blade pulling out covered in bright blood.

People found the damndest weapons when an apocalypse struck.

I raised my rifle to shoot, but Gabe stepped in, shoving him against the hard wall. His head snapped back and she cracked his neck, then he slid down to the floor. Once he was down, she kicked his sides hard before popping a bullet in his head.

That was another of Gabe's redeeming moments.

"I had a bone to pick with him," she said as she sized me up with glittering blue eyes.

He was a rapist and she was a woman. I didn't need clarification.

The sound of shots and screams echoed down the hall. I hoped Frank and Blaze were on the winning side of whatever was going on. Part of me wanted to help, but I had to rescue Pickle while I could.

We made it to the kitchen. It was huge. It had to be to feed a building packed with inmates. Animals were caged everywhere. Cats, dogs, and some traditional farmhouse animals looked forlornly at us. I was a heartless bastard when it came to humans, but the sight of them all waiting to be eaten disturbed me. The mammals had a chance outside. Zombies didn't eat them.

I found Pickle first, caged with a couple other rodents, including a chinchilla. She was overwhelmed to see me, and eagerly scurried up my arm and onto my shoulder. I didn't have a backpack on, and her being in the open concerned me. Holding her with one hand, I unlocked cages as fast as I could, cutting open the ones I couldn't.

Between unlocking the cages of a pig and a Labrador, I searched the kitchen for a way out. Based on the exit sign above the door at the end of the hall and our location, I decided the door was the other loading dock.

Gabe unlocked the exit and herded the animals outside. The pig ran towards the light, and every animal we released followed.

As I unlocked the last cage, the swinging kitchen doors burst open. Our missing comrades saw the open exit and ran for it.

"Come on, Cyrus!" Frank said as he passed me.

Faint shouts and voices were coming from outside the kitchen. We didn't have enough ammo to take out the horde that must've been on its way. Their numbers would overwhelm us once we ran outside. I scanned the kitchen, looking for anything useful.

Then I saw it.

The footsteps of our enemy grew louder, echoing down the hall. They were yelling scriptures fanatically, screaming about avenging their lunatic leader's death. All normal conversation for crazies.

Frank and Gabe yelling for me to hurry up almost distracted me from unscrewing the propane tank. Since the door was open, we could've made a run for it, but they'd still be on our trail. If my plan worked, the kitchen exit would be unusable, and the crazies would have to deal with a prison on fire.

Pushing my luck and ignoring my companions, I set the tank in front of the entrance and turned my back. Gabe was gone, but Frank moved towards me. Couldn't he put two and two together? The explosion from the propane tank would be severe; no one who wanted to live should be anywhere near it went I shot.

"What the fuck are you doing? Run!"

They were behind me. I heard the entrance open, knocking the tank on its side. They were at the opposite end of the kitchen, but that didn't matter to bullets. Frank finally disappeared through the door, but Blaze was yards away from it. I saw her bend down behind a steel counter, reach for something, almost lose it. I thought she was capable, but whatever she was doing proved me wrong.

By the time I got to the exit, Blaze was there too. She was halfway out the door when I pushed her to the left against the outside wall. I pivoted on my foot just outside of the doorway, my body slamming into hers. As I spun 180 degrees, the kitchen came back into view. Crazies were in clear sight, getting ready to fire, unaware of the hazard in front of them. It only took a second to aim and shoot the tank just a few feet in front of them.

Everything happened at once. The door beside us flew off its hinges from the force of the explosion, landing in overgrown grass. Heat washed over me, making my eyes hurt and my skin tight. The impact shook the thick stone wall we used as cover, and pebbles and dust burst from its cracks.

The explosion happened quickly, but the aftermath was what hurt the most. My ears were ringing and my head felt fuzzy. Smoke billowed from the kitchen. I coughed as I inhaled. Pieces of fiery debris caught the browned grass on fire; some areas were already beyond control.

From inside came agonizing screams. The explosion would've killed all the crazies I saw, but if my prediction was right there would've been even more headed for the hallway. The flames and impact would've kept traveling in every direction, hitting them too, but some less severely.

I'd been holding onto Blaze. I released her, taking a shaky step back.

The ragged brick wall hit my face as someone pushed me from behind. I felt my skin tearing as the stone dug in.

Pressure on my shoulder made me turn my head. A tremendously overcooked face snarled, and its blackened teeth tried to latch onto me. His skin crackled, while the smell of oily, burnt fat filled my nostrils. Lips were long gone, and his teeth gnashed furiously. I tried using the wall as leverage to push us both back, but he had been a big fucker before he died. He weighed too much and moved too violently.

This one was a runner. It dug its hands into my shoulders, trying to pull me closer. Its strength was no more than it was when it was living, but the determination in its oozing, grip made up for it. The smoldering zombie pushed me back against the wall just as I was gaining leverage, my head spinning as it hit.

She was there then. Blaze was fast, pushing the thing off me. It stumbled then lurched forward towards me. A bullet went through the middle of its forehead. Boiled brains spewed from the exit hole and the body fell.

My strength came back as I stepped away from the wall. I felt my face, and my hand came away with blood after I pressed my fingers into the throbbing wound. A stinging, sharp sensation reminded me my shoulder was sliced up. Everything was going downhill. We had to get out of there.

If there were more runners, they weren't coming outside. Frank and Gabe stood near the red Mustang we'd seen earlier, their eyes fixated on the doorway.

I paid attention to my surroundings. Moans and groans filled the air, but they weren't coming from inside. I wasn't sure if the night brought out the dead, or if it was the ruckus inside the prison that drew them, but they were here in all their slimy, undead glory. The stench of rot was overwhelming, and I almost choked when I inhaled. Sunny weather made corpses extra juicy and pungent.

"This is mine. Get in," Blaze said as she walked to the Mustang.

All of us were frazzled, but we were regrouping faster than I thought.

Frank said, "We have a Hummer up front."

"Just get in. I'll take you."

We were still in a hot zone, so I didn't argue. I wanted to blame the impact of the explosion for rattling my mind, but since everyone else was fine I couldn't. Frank slid into the backseat with Gabe and I got into the front.

The Mustang smelled like old leather and tobacco. There was a pack of cigarettes on the floor of the front seat. Empty cigarette boxes littered the dashboard.

"This is yours," she said as she dropped an angry, squirming ferret in my lap. "Don't thank me. I'm not interested."

My mouth hung open. I couldn't say I word.

She turned the car on, while all of us remained silent.

Chapter 12

The Hummer was untouched. I was surprised, since I thought any insane rapists left alive might use it to escape. As we drew closer to it, and the entrance of the prison, the area remained empty.

My time with Blaze was drawing to a close. Since she had a car, there was no logical reason she'd want to stay with us. She pulled the Mustang alongside the Hummer, keeping her foot on the brake instead of parking it. I opened the door and pushed the seat forward so Frank and Gabe could exit.

We all turned our heads when we heard the faint echo of a gunshot from within the prison.

I handed Pickle to Frank who took her into the Hummer, leaving Blaze and me alone. I wasn't ready for our time to finish. There were only a few people on Earth, most of which were probably dead, who I found interesting. Blaze was…

"Cyrus! Let's go!"

I glared at Gabe for the interruption. She sunk back into the cushioned backseat before slamming the door shut. Through the window, I saw Frank looking anywhere but at me.

"We're going east," I said. "We've got a cache of guns and supplies in the Hummer, and a safe destination."

Blaze's eyebrows rose, but I didn't think she was surprised. Her expression made me feel like a toddler.

"Follow us until you have a better plan," I said.

"Alright."

"Boy," came Frank's voice.

Gabe I could ignore, but when Frank used that tone it meant "Get in the Hummer right now, or else." He was right. I was acting like we were out of danger.

I tried not to act giddy as I shut the Mustang door and hopped into the Hummer.

"Is she coming with us?" Gabe asked.

"Yes."

Gabe opened her door and got out.

"Where do you think you're going?"

"I'm riding with her. Why would I stay with you if I have a choice?"

She wanted to have girl time with Blaze. Call it a hunch, but I didn't think Blaze was the kind of woman who would like that. Before I could stop her, she got in the front seat and slammed the door shut.

I started the Hummer and drove until I found the front gates of the prison. They were shut, but not many stiffs were in front. Frank volunteered to open it, and left me alone before I could object. I watched as he walked to the gate, noticing a limp I hadn't before.

As he got closer, three Zs lined up in front of him. He pulled out his handgun and shot each in the head before pushing the gate open.

"Let's go to the gas station and regroup," Frank said once back in the vehicle.

"Fine"

Backtracking wasn't my favorite thing to do, but the gas station was the only place we could go to rest. I was running on adrenaline. My wounds needed cleaning, but my highest priority was to eat and remain stationary until I felt up to moving again.

The gas station had a few new visitors. We debated and decided to park the car behind the pumps closest to the building. It was close, but partially blocked from the street. Blaze parked her car at the entrance of the parking lot, drawing the Zs who'd gathered around us away so we could handle them. After a brief dispatch of some shambling zombies, the four of us went in. The doors had bolts on the top and bottom, which we engaged, offering us mild protection or warning against intruders.

I roamed the aisles looking for anything nutritionally acceptable. There was no point in eating any of my MREs since there was sustenance readily available. With heavy resignation, I settled on a couple of energy bars, washing it all down with a bottle of Aquafina.

Blaze and Gabe sat on the floor behind the register, apart and clearly uncomfortable. Frank read the back of a bag of chips. Tired, I sat down between the girls, working on the chewy mass of granola bar.

Females were strange. While I couldn't pinpoint exactly why, I felt nervous around Gabe and Blaze. Even though neither spoke, I felt a current of negativity between the two. I wondered what transpired in the car on their ride over. Whatever it was, they seemed pissed at each other. And I put myself right between them.

Cyrus V. Sinclair. The V stands for vacant. As in my mind is vacant of logical thought. Well, it makes sense to me.

"We need to find somewhere more secure for the night," I said.

Frank, who opted for a piece of jerky instead of the chips, said, "Take a breather. I reckon no one in that prison is coming out alive, and if any do they won't be in any state to look for us."

Blaze didn't have a problem taking a breather. She had already shifted into a more comfortable position and her breathing grew shallow. I figured it was from her time in the marines. She could sleep on command because she had to.

Gabe bit her lip and glared at her, then at me. She was having issues and wanted to talk, but I wasn't in the mood to deal with her, especially after everything at the prison.

After I forced down the rest of my food, I stretched onto the cold ground, glad the counter offered us invisibility from the front of the store. We were safer that way, and it made me feel a little more at ease.

Frank and Gabe didn't appear to be as ready to fall asleep. Neither was I. But, despite my minds protests, I was worn out and fell asleep soon.

* * *

I woke up stiff and groggy. My head and shoulder protested to the nth degree as I sat up and tried to work the knots out of my muscles. An angry, throbbing headache had brewed while I slept, and it worked full force to make my life hell.

It was barely dusk. Rain drizzled outside. I smelled cigarette smoke, and glanced over at Blaze, who had one hanging from her lips. Her eyes were shadowed in the dim light, but the tip of her cigarette burned brightly whenever she inhaled, illuminating them. She looked calm and casual, just sitting there with her knees up and one arm slung across them. In front of her stood a fort made of stacked cigarette boxes.

Gabe was curled in a fetal position, out stone cold. She breathed deeply, her face blank with the bliss of sleep. Maybe she'd be in a cranky mood, too, when she woke up, then I wouldn't be alone in my misery. Frank was the farthest away from us, his back pressed against the counter. He was asleep.

"Sun's going to be down in about half hour. We should leave soon," Blaze said, her voice low.

I nodded as I brought myself up into a cross-legged position. My mind buzzed in tandem with a prickling traveling across my skin. "How long have we been out?"

"Not long," she said. "Maybe an hour. I woke up a few minutes ago."

It felt like I'd been unconscious for weeks. We needed to find somewhere to sleep and regroup. I was about to speak when Blaze beat me to it.

"You want me to take care of her?" She jerked her head toward Gabe's sleeping form.

"Take care of her?"

"Smoke her."

Well, I thought, *that's awfully blunt.*

This woman was offering to murder Gabe. Although I wasn't sure of her reason, it was a good offer. Gabe was becoming increasingly difficult to work with, but was death a fair punishment? Maybe just leaving her behind was better.

"Why?"

"I see the way she acts towards you. Emotional attachments make accomplishing tasks difficult, can muddle your decision-making abilities. You know, I haven't known her for long, but if I were in charge, she wouldn't be here right now."

"I'm not attached, and I'm not in charge."

Blaze's face reflected mild amusement. "I never said you were. It's all on her part. She's a loose cannon and could slow us down. Maybe even compromise us."

I realized she'd been with Gabe in the prison cell. That and the car ride were enough to absorb Gabe's overall personality.

Her points were valid, but I wasn't ready to kill Gabe just yet. She could be useful in getting us to our final location. Or was I justifying? I didn't think so.

"I'll tell you what. We'll make a decision once we find somewhere to sleep. I can't think straight right now."

I wondered if Blaze saw this as a sign of weakness, and I tried to tell myself it didn't matter too much what she thought of me. With a barely noticeable nod, she agreed.

Outside I heard muffled voices. I looked at Blaze and raised my brows.

"Four living humans," she said. "They're siphoning gas and considering breaking into the Hummer."

Great.

"How close to breaking in are they?" I whispered, mind already racing for a way to handle this. The situation might not need to be handled if they just went on their way, but that was unlikely if they spotted our formidable cache of weapons.

"One of them is circling it and looking in. He doesn't want the alarm to go off. He seems afraid."

The world was overrun with zombies. No one was alive. There was nothing to lose. If I were them, I'd take my chances and break in. Maybe they didn't know how to hotwire it or were just stupid. I'd never be caught dead making decisions like these people were.

Blaze snuffed her cigarette and moved into a crouched position so she could look over the counter. The staccato sound of rapid fire interrupted her just as she was about to speak.

"Some runners and slows are surrounding them from multiple directions. I'm not sure how we should proceed."

Her last sentence didn't sound too convincing, as though she already had a plan formed but wasn't sure I'd agree. Stiffly, I moved into a prone position and picked my rifle up from beside me.

"I'm sure you've got some ideas."

Blaze's grin revealed a chipped right canine. It gave her character.

Wide-eyed and confused, Gabe awakened with the gunfire. Frank was awake, but didn't look concerned. Apparently, we were all ready to go.

"I say we run out, get in the Hummer, and go. Eliminate any opposition" Blaze said, clearly trying to keep the eager bloodlust out of her voice.

"Okay. Sounds good."

Gabe snapped at us. "What the fuck is going on here?"

"Just stay behind us," I said. "There's a threat outside."

"I'll go first," Blaze insisted. "Cover my six."

She made her way to the door, unlocking it smoothly before pushing it open, gun on the ready. I followed her, but gave her a suitable amount of distance.

Outside, the light was all dim and blue. Since it was summer, I guessed it was around 9p.m. Mist hung thick in the air, limiting visibility and dampening my hands even through my gloves. Muzzles flashed by the gas pumps, lighting the form of a big truck. Crazed, jerking movements easily set the runners apart from the humans. Identifying zombies wasn't a chore.

Breathing in the humid air, I focused on the glum task at hand. The survivors were all men and had each other's backs covered. They were stupid. Firing wildly in the middle of a gas station was a sure way to get killed.

"Army guys!" one of them shouted.

We were spotted.

"Help us!" another chimed in.

I guess we did look like military, since we were so thoroughly decked out in tactical gear. Blaze even wore a camo flak jacket with the nametag.

None of us answered, but from behind me Gabe opened fire on a runner that was charging us. We were at the Hummer, and the ragged men stared at us expectantly. Blaze took a defensive stance. Mimicking her, Gabe took out undead who were getting too close. Frank let the girls handle the shooting while he kept a broader lookout. I assumed that made me leader, which meant I had to deal with the survivor issue.

"Thanks," an older, graying man said. "We thought we were done for."

Blaze opened fire, blowing the brains out of a shambling, fat woman. Gabe shot a teenage girl in the leg, then re-aimed and shot her in the head.

"We can't help you," I said. "Get in your truck and go."

"W-what?" His three companions glanced over at us. "We need to stick together. I mean, you can't just leave us!"

Desperation and guns were a terrible mix. This guy and his friends had both factors playing against them. Slowly I backed up to the driver's side of the Hummer and fished the keys out of my back pocket. I hit the unlock button twice. The lights flashed and Gabe, Blaze, and Frank got into the front and backseats.

"These fuckers ain't gonna help us, Steven! Get in the truck," shouted a gnarly redneck of a man.

Steven appeared to be close to a breakdown. He barely held onto the shotgun in his shaking hands, and his lip quivered. I guess I traumatized him or something. In my defense, it wasn't like I promised to be his savior.

From inside the car, Blaze leaned over the passenger side and pushed the door open. "Let's move."

The men looked agitated, unsure if we were a more worthy enemy than the zombies. I took my chance and leapt into the driver's seat.

"You're awful," Steven screamed, lifting his shotgun at me.

As he pulled the trigger his arm jerked up, and he shot the top part of the window, missing me entirely. Thousands of miniscule pieces of glass burst into the vehicle, filling crevices and getting in my clothes.

What caused his misfire? A little girl had sunk her teeth into his side, vigorously chomping through his flesh. Blonde pigtails and a pink dress made the scene comic, but I didn't have time to laugh. With their weak leader gone, the living men tried to make it for the truck, but the undead had become numerous.

"Let's move," Blaze said. "We're surrounded."

So we did. Zombies—slow and fast—made their inevitable way toward the Hummer. Most of them saw the other guys scrambling for the truck as an easier target, but a few noticed we were canned goods.

Get it? Canned goods? Because we were in the car?

Anyway...

I rammed the key into the ignition and the car roared to life. A few unfortunate Zs were in the way, so I ran them over as I turned hard back onto the main road. The rearview mirror showed carnage unfolding on the unwise survivors. Well, they weren't survivors anymore.

"We'll come back for your car," I told Blaze. "It isn't safe now."

"I agree."

"Well, that didn't go well," Gabe said from the backseat.

"Most people aren't meant to survive," Blaze said. "They gave their position away and brought it on themselves."

Gabe snorted. "We could have helped them. If we covered them, they could've gotten into the truck."

Though Gabe couldn't see it, Blaze's upper lip twitched, making the scar across her face look uglier than normal. Her feelings were transparent at that moment.

I answered for her. "They were losing it. Even if we covered them, that Steven guy had already lost it. I don't know if you noticed, but he tried to shoot me."

Silence from the backseat, then, "The other three…"

Blaze jerked her head to the side, glared hard at Gabe. I looked back to the road, leaving it to them to work the fight out.

"You or a stranger?" Wright asked.

"What?"

"You don't seem to value your life. Would you die for a group of strangers who were at their end?"

"They weren't—"

"It doesn't matter. Right now, and for the rest of our lives, it's always going to be you or them. If you stayed, you would've died trying to protect them."

"You two would've—"

"No, we would not have stayed. Cyrus and Frank don't care about them and neither do I. Which brings us to the original question: you or a stranger?"

Gabe breathed deeply in anger. I glanced in the mirror and saw her clenching her jaw so hard I could swear I heard it. Frank looked tired.

"Well, aren't you two fucking perfect for each other," she said, telling us off in any way she could, like a teenager scorned by her mother.

Battle won, Blaze faced forward, an uncharacteristically pleased look on her face.

Chapter 13

We drove a short distance down the main drag before returning to the gas station. There were no sign of the living. Quite a few stiffs roamed around, but none were close to Blaze's Mustang. Before she left, I gave her the shortwave radio I'd given Gabe the day before, so we could communicate without leaving the cars. Gabe, unaware of Blaze's disgust for her, got into the Mustang, too.

The right side of my face was sticky and itchy with blood. I needed to find time to check my shoulder wound to make sure it wasn't already infected. My feet were killing me. How I wanted to take my boots off. I hadn't done so since Gabe and I left the apartment in Seattle. A tiny, infuriating itch terrorized the arch of my foot.

Undead hands reached out from open car windows as we drove. Some of them close enough I heard their bloody fingertips scratching against the side of the vehicle. The driver's side window was broken, forcing me to make wide turns away from anything on my side.

We passed the prison and were in new territory.

I stopped the vehicle in front of a junior high. Its gates were closed, but hundreds of undead adolescents pressed up against the chain link fence, trying to claw their way out. For a moment, I marveled in the melancholy of it all. Maybe one undead got in and bit someone while they were trying to shut the school down. That's all it took: one bite.

Bumping caught my attention. I leaned out the window and looked down. A drooling, white-eyed toddler banged against my door. There was a substantial chunk of neck missing and a cascade of old, coagulated blood down his chest. I looked away. While I was zoning out, staring at the mass of dead kids, my radio hissed.

"Cyrus. Why did you stop? Over."

I grabbed it and clicked the transmit button. "I'm fine, Blaze. Just assessing. Over."

"What's the plan? Over."

"Keep heading east for Highway 2. It's at the end of town. Over."

We only made it another ten minutes before disaster struck again.

The wreckage lessened, and our cars navigated around the remaining junk with ease. After the junior high there were some houses and a terrifying nursing home, but nothing too traumatizing. Houses were destroyed or unscathed, and occasional rotting figures lay on the ground. Our windows were shut, but I knew well what the festering scents were like.

I noticed a sign proclaiming Main Street, which meant we were right on track. Right on track was a temporary term. Just as we got up to an intersection, the Mustang veered off to the right onto a residential street, then halted with a piercing screech. I followed, Frank and I staring at the red car, waiting for something to happen.

Frank picked up the radio and called them. No reply.

Gabe practically fell from the passenger's side, and only a quick grab of the car door saved her from a face plant. In a more dignified manner, Blaze threw open the other side and strode with a purpose around the vehicle. Her fists were clenched and her mouth was set in a grim line. I knew what was coming.

Blaze's first punch landed right into Gabe's ribcage. She stumbled back, doubling over, before using her low stance to ram Blaze up against the car. I watched as Blaze's head hit the window, temporarily stunning her. Gabe rammed a fist into Blaze's stomach, but that was the last shot she got in.

Fights were short in reality, and Blaze made sure of this. With a good show of brute strength, she shoved off Gabe. She let the momentum of the move carry her into a kick a black belt would appreciate. Her foot hit Gabe in the center of her chest and effectively knocked her onto the ground.

As Gabe tried to get up, Blaze lost some of her cool and threw a sloppy kick into her side. It did damage, but wasn't as precise as her previous kick. My mouth dropped open when Blaze continued to kick Gabe.

"Boy, you'd better do something about that," Frank said.

Why me? Why was I the one who had to mediate everything? Why was I the one who had to deal with everyone's psychotic breakdowns?

None too happy, I roughly shoved the car door open and ran over to Blaze. I came up behind her and threw my arms around her waist, hauling the wild woman off Gabe. She tried to bolt out of my grasp but, ignoring my protesting shoulders, I squeezed tighter until I knew it hurt.

"Let me go," Blaze said, her calm voice contradicting her struggle to get free.

"No." I walked backwards, creating distance between her and her prey.

Frank passed me and went to Gabe, giving the battered girl a hand up. Blood poured from her nose and mouth, while she clutched her midsection. Frank guided her to the Hummer and helped her in before taking the wheel himself.

After coercing Blaze into the Mustang and finding ourselves sitting in silence, I let a shaky laugh escape.

"You really got her."

Blaze got out of the fight without a busted lip or nose. Of course, I'd imagine the back of her head was throbbing and her stomach was tight, but beyond that, she was the evident victor. I remembered my fight in the apartment with Gabe, and how she fared a little better with me. A disturbing thought crossed my mind: Blaze could probably beat me silly.

"Couldn't finish the job fast enough," she said in that monotone voice. My gaze caught hers. "Let's find somewhere to sleep. Then we'll have that talk."

I did promise Blaze we'd discuss the Gabe issue. The more I thought about it, the more I realized how biased I'd become toward Blaze, who I knew drastically less about her than Gabe. That didn't matter, though. Blaze proved more useful and lucid than Gabe.

Shutting away the conflicting thoughts, I started to answer but stopped. I didn't know what we were going to do about Gabe. Nothing really needed to be done. Just because they didn't get along, and because I didn't like her, didn't mean we could just kill her. I knew Blaze felt quite differently, but I wasn't ready to be the partner of a murderous psychopath just yet.

"I'm responsible for her," I said, adding, "I guess," to make it seem more casual.

Blaze looked skeptical. "Responsible." She shook her head. "I thought you were better than that."

I shrugged, about to spit out a very good comeback, when another explosion rumbled down the road. This time it was way too close for comfort. I snatched up the radio and called Frank.

"You there?" I noticed Blaze muttered "over" when I didn't.

"'Course I am, boy."

"That sounded close..."

"Yee-ah, it did. I reckon it might be some crazies, you know? I think we should hide ourselves and wait for a while."

"I agree. No zombies around this area. Let's take advantage of that. You lead the way. Find a house that looks safe."

The Hummer shuddered to life, and I followed it down the road it veered onto. A few minutes later, Frank pulled into the driveway of a rambler. The garage was open, and there was no fence guarding the backyard. He drove the Hummer around the side of the house, parking it next to a stagnant swimming pool.

I did the same. We all stayed still in our cars, listening.

From across town, a loud engine approached. Many engines, I realized, as the sound grew closer. Soon they passed by us, but all the motors shut off instead of fading away. Whoever the group was, they were stopping for the day. It was hard to say what the explosions were, but they could've been intentional. Humans were difficult adversaries, and I wasn't interested in fighting a horde of them.

As quietly as I could, I got out of the Hummer, grabbing my pack before shutting the door. Blaze, Frank, and Gabe did the same. Moving as one, we went to the front of the house and slid in through the garage. The door was shut but unlocked.

Frank took initiative and lowered the garage door, which wasn't automatic. The sound was louder than I preferred, but the shut door offered more protection.

Blaze brought her rifle up and took point, searching the house. I waited with the other two at the garage entrance. A couple bloody prints adorned walls and floors and around the door, but everything else was normal.

She came back with her gun pointing down, an indicator the house was clear. Just as she was about to open her mouth, the lights flickered on. That sector of the city was being powered for a few hours, and I was excited. Electricity was convenient, though at the moment I couldn't think of anything to do with it.

An angry Gabe pushed passed us and into the living space, shooting Blaze daggers as she went.

The house was an older single story home with dark brown carpet and brown paneled wood walls. There was a master bedroom with an attached bathroom, a guest bedroom, and a bigger living space that was all adjoined. Overall, the house was in flawless condition, as though the original owners just left for a quick trip.

"Blaze, we need to talk," I said, as Frank and Gabe fell onto the living room sofa.

She turned to face me, an expectant expression on her face. Regardless of her emotions, if she really had any, she followed me into the master bedroom. I shut the door behind us. My newfound sense of guilt made me feel like I hadn't discussed the fight between her and Gabe thoroughly enough.

"What happened with Gabe? You could've gotten us killed."

Her brows came together and she scowled at me, but stayed silent. I shrugged my pack off and took Pickle out so she could get some air and exercise. When I sat on the bed, Blaze leaned against the wall in front of me.

"She got on my nerves. I had to put her in her place. Why are we talking about this again?"

Like I hadn't heard that before, and I told her so. "When I met Gabe, I beat the hell out of her, but it only changed her attitude for a couple days. She gets on my nerves every second of her existence, but—"

"We finished this talk in the car, Dad. But since you want to do it again, here, you compromise when you shouldn't, Sinclair. That girl contributes nothing—"

"She can shoot. She isn't as bad as you think."

"Oh, really? How many times have you seen her shoot a gun? She's tagging along because she'd die otherwise. She can't go solo."

I shook my head. "That's not true. She was on her own before she came to me."

Blaze shook her head. Her almost-black eyes pierced right through me, and I shifted uncomfortably. "No, she was not. Back at the prison, I heard her talking to the warden's daughter. The building she was staying in wasn't secure. Zs got in and killed some of the group she was staying with. When she came running down your street, she was trying to escape whatever clusterfuck she left behind. She was trying to find someone else. Probably someone stronger and better suited to take care of a teenage girl.

"Fuck, Sinclair. None of those guns or gear were even hers. She got caught up in a gang and they used her for sex. Those guys you ran into? They were sent by her pimp leader to scoop her back up for currency in their safe house. Every shot, every punch—it was all out of luck."

Why did Gabe make it all up? To make herself look tough? It wouldn't surprise me. Really, it made sense for her to make up an entirely new identity in this chaotic world. She wanted to come off as relentless and strong. If anything, I had to give her credit for the elaborate ruse she managed to pull on me. I felt duped, which I certainly wasn't used to.

"Ah," was all I could manage.

Blaze pushed herself off the wall and sat down next to me. "She lied to you. What are you going to do about it?"

I turned to face her and glared. "Why am I the unofficial leader of our fucked up parade?"

She shrugged. "Maybe when you decided to unofficially make choices for Frank and Gabe. When you unofficially saved their lives. You're a hero. It's disgusting."

"What about you? I haven't done anything for you, but you're here."

"I'm using you. I need to go east for a while, and I know you're capable of getting me there. When you told me where you were headed, I decided to take advantage of it."

"You think you're going to stay with us?"

"Us?"

We looked at each other blankly. What was she implying?

She grinned, showing that cracked canine. I didn't know what was funny, so I remained devoid of emotion.

"You really think we're all going to make it?" Behind her words, I detected a threat.

"I guess not. I know I will. I never considered the rest of you."

"You're not unstoppable." Blaze got up and walked to the door, leaving me alone and full of thought.

* * *

When the undead craze started, I was a different person. Cold, calculated. I took pride in how much of an icy bastard I could be. As I started saving people, I started giving a damn. Just a little damn, almost insignificant, but it changed me. First with Gabe, then I let Blaze Wright in for the ride. The only person I was comfortable caring about was Frank. Everyone else was an abnormality. My old self would consider the new self a complete idiot, a failure. I disagreed. I wasn't that far gone.

Having people rely on me wasn't what I had planned. Somehow, I let Gabe convince me, and my policy changed entirely. How did I let that happen? How could a barely-adult, screwed up liar of a girl convince the great Cyrus V. Sinclair to do anything?

The V stands for versatility, I guess. Heaven knows I'd been compromising and versatile with my plans.

I let my gaze wander around the nondescript room. Queen bed with a navy blue comforter. Walk in closet, chest of drawers. Night stands. One of them even had an old glass of water on it. While I stared at the glass, my vision went out of focus. Blaze was right. Not all of us would make it. Most of my conscience wanted only me to make it, and maybe Frank. No, that was selfish. Frank was the reason the plan existed. Frank could make it, but Blaze? Gabe?

The women were unnecessary, and no matter how much I defended her, Blaze was right about Gabe. She was a loose cannon and would be a nightmare to live with. Hell, she was a nightmare no matter what the circumstances.

And Blaze? Black hair, long nose, dark eyes, scar on her right cheek, cigarette pressed between her lips. Many words fit her: efficient, callous, badass. She'd be useful in surviving, but I knew she'd kill me without a nanosecond of hesitation if she wanted to. In fact, I'd bet she'd leave me to an agonizing death-by-zombie if it granted her a few extra minutes of escape time.

I admired her ruthlessness and, honestly, aspired to be like that. It would make surviving in an undead world a lot easier.

However, surviving had been easy so far, so did it even matter? We had a gas-guzzling behemoth loaded with weapons, ammunition, and food. Resources weren't an issue. The only issue was the conflict in the group I was surviving with.

I thought about how good Orange Hi-C tasted with Sour Patch kids. Talk about a delightful sugar rush. I'd have to raid a convenience store if it was…well, convenient. Just because most of the world happened to be living dead didn't mean I'd skimp on what I liked.

As long as the situation didn't worsen, everything would work out. Even if the players didn't get along, we still had better odds than most people out there. We weren't afraid of the undead and we could defend ourselves. What more could someone ask for?

Scratch that question. I knew what other people would ask for. The zombies to disappear, life to return to normal, what have you.

Good thing I wasn't other people.

Chapter 14

After pondering my existence a while longer, I left the bedroom to find the rest of them sitting around in the living room. Blaze and Frank sat in silence on a beige couch patterned with golden leaves and flowers. I wasn't shocked to see Gabe sitting in an armchair across from them looking anywhere but at us. She was angry and I couldn't blame her.

I sat between the veterans and propped my feet on the coffee table. To the side of my boots was *Better Homes and Gardens* with a glorious chocolate cake on its cover. Every part of me craved that confection the moment I saw it.

No one was speaking. It was nice to zone out and forget about killing, escaping, surviving, and anything related to those verbs and just stare at a magazine cover It was becoming harder to clear my mind as the days went by.

"What were ya'll doing when you found out?" Frank asked.

Our heads turned. The women stared at him like he was crazy, and I would've too, if I didn't know any better. Frank loved a good story, and now seemed like a fitting time to share.

Frank knew my story, and it wasn't spectacular, but it would break the ice.

"I was at work," I said.

"Where did you work?" Gabe interrupted.

"24-hour Walgreens. I was a pharmacist working graveyard shift."

Gabe snickered. "I figured you'd do something more evil. Like killing baby animals or evicting people."

Ignoring her, I continued. "I was working with another guy named Rick. It was probably two in the morning, so there wasn't anyone in the store. Just a teenage kid figuring out what kind of condom to buy. Doors slid open and this woman shuffled in. She was white with a kind of blue undertone. I didn't give her more than a glance, because I never look at the customers. Rick was on his break, and I was encased in the pharmacy section of the store. It's the kind that's all decked out with hard plastic. Probably bullet proof.

"I was sucking on a mouthful of cherry Jolly Ranchers, and I went back to separating the rest of the flavors. Then I heard the Condom Kid yelling. The woman grabbed at him and he kept pushing her away. She bit him on the arm. Her neck was chewed out and some of her face. The kid started gushing blood. I called the cops.

"One thing I knew back when things were normal was to never get in the way. I didn't know she was a zombie. I didn't have time to think about it. It's not like you see something like that and go, 'Yeah, living dead right there.' But I did know if I killed her and played hero, I'd probably go to jail for it. Never mind she was trying to eat that kid. He ran out of the store and she followed him. Ten minutes later the cops showed up, I explained what happened, then took off the rest of the night.

"That was the last night I worked. I knew something was wrong. It all felt cliché, like in horror movies. I went home and everything happened. The news, power failure, total chaos. I left a few times to stock up on supplies, but that was it."

My story ended on a boring note, just like it started. Not everyone had to have an epic story of how they found out zombies were real, how they survived and coped with it.

A memory of my childhood popped up. There was a series of books for teenagers at the library called "Coping With." Coping with divorce, coping with anxiety. I wondered if twenty years into the future there was going to be a "Coping with zombies" or "Coping with killing your undead relatives and friends."

"I'd just gotten back from my second tour in Iraq," Blaze said, her voice distant and a little dreamy. "I had nowhere to go because I'd been in the military for so long. So, I went to my half-sister's house. She needed someone to watch her son, Joey, and said I could live there if I took care of him. Just until I figured things out for myself."

I pictured Blaze Wright as a different person pre-Zombie era. When she spoke of her previous life she even sounded different—a little less cold and unmoved.

"I lived there for a few weeks before news of some new virus caught wind. Carolyn, my half-sister, was bitten and went straight to the hospital. The TV said people were typically quarantined for a few days. She told me to take care of Joey until she got back. I agreed, because what else was I going to do?

"Anyway, I woke up and went downstairs. The front door was wide open. Joey was eight and had a tendency to let himself out to play in the front yard. He'd never shut the door no matter how angry his mom and I got. When I went to close it, I heard noises in the kitchen. You know. The chewing noises they make when they're eating.

"I shut the door and locked it before going into the kitchen. The neighbor, Bill, was eating Joey. His stomach was ripped up like a grenade got to him. Blood was everywhere. Bill didn't notice me. I knew what he was. I didn't have a hard time believing things like that. I picked up Carolyn's cast iron pan out of the dish rack and beat his head in. Joey started twitching while I was doing that, so I crushed his skull, too.

"I didn't have many things. I went upstairs and packed my sack and got my gun out of the closet. I just had a little 9mm and a couple of extra clips. I had no idea where to go, but I figured I owed it to Carolyn to tell her about Joey. Maybe save her. If I hadn't been so stupid, I would've realized a hospital was the worst place to go."

Blaze shook her head. "That's another story, though. The hospital and everything after."

Frank looked unusually sympathetic towards her. "How did you end up at the prison?"

Her eyes gleamed with rage. "I had the Mustang at that point. When I got to Monroe, I stopped at a roadblock they'd created. They jumped me. I killed two of them.

"It's all so funny. Right when Carolyn left for the hospital she said to me, 'Bea, you're almost thirty and you have no kids, no husband. What's it going to take for you to find that? The end of the world?' I guess she was wrong, though. End of the world and still no kids, no husband."

Gabe piped in. "Did you even want that? A couple of kids, a demeaning husband?"

Every once in a while, Gabe suppressed her stupidity and said something insightful. This was one of those times. Blaze looked at her and shook her head.

"I can't have kids. I got a hysterectomy before I went into the military. As for a husband...most men I've met don't like the fact I have bigger balls than they do."

We all chuckled. It was true about her being overly masculine. I couldn't imagine any normal man wanting to be with a woman who could handle herself better than he could. Most men wanted to protect their women, but Blaze didn't need protecting. I liked that about her.

Frank turned to Gabe. "What about you, firecracker?"

Blaze's face went blank, and I forced my face to do the same. After what she had just told me, I wanted to kill Gabe for her dishonesty.

"I don't have a story. It just happened."

I was expecting her to lie and make up some half-assed story about the East Coast and her assassin past. When she didn't, I wasn't sure what was going on. She told me the tale easily enough. Maybe it was because she knew Blaze knew the truth? Or she just wasn't in the mood to talk. I wasn't sure.

Out of habit, I patted down my vest pockets, just to take inventory of what I had. One pocket had a familiar box in it. I pulled out a fun-size container of Dots.

Score, Cyrus.

Frank, keen on keeping the ball rolling, launched into his story. I chewed on stale sugar dots and listened.

"Well, I've been living down in Little Rock since as long as I can remember. Then I got antsy and moved up here to Washington, up in the mountains. Built me my cabin, real good. Then, when I was in town, I heard about the virus and whatnot. I wondered how Cyrus was doing, so I packed a bag an' made my way to Seattle."

"How did you know where I was? I didn't tell you when I left Little Rock."

"Tracked you down," was his reply. Apparently, that part of the story wasn't up for discussion.

Stillness filled the room again, leaving everyone to their own thoughts.

Moments later Gabe spoke, asking a question that was in the back of our minds. "Why do you think some of them are fast? Why don't they stay that way?"

Frank and I both shrugged. As of late, I didn't have time to consider many whys.

"The warden had a theory," Blaze said. "She thought it had to do with rigor mortis. It doesn't set in for a few hours, which is about how long the zombies can run. Once it sets in, they're slow."

"It makes sense," I said. "Everything starts decomposing after death. Once rigor goes away, the decomposition is probably grave enough to make them slow."

Once a few more theories were shared, we stopped talking. There were things to consider. Our plan of action, for one. Monroe was teeming with life, more so than Seattle had been. The cars we heard earlier might be driven by hostiles, just like the men at the prison. Heaven knew I didn't want to run into a fiasco like that again. Even if they were good Samaritans, I'd rather not deal with it.

Frank pulled out a map from his coat pocket . He spread it out on the coffee table in front of us and we found our location. We mapped out a way across to the next town. So far, the highways and freeways had been drivable, but if there were a safer, less populated way to get to Sultan, there would be no plausible reason not to take it.

I voiced my thoughts to the group.

"We were on West Main Street before we pulled off," I said, setting my finger on the road. "I guess we took a right about here at Morris Street."

After some careful analysis, we decided there were three ways to get out of town. The first was to take Highway 2 due east, but that didn't seem like a good idea. Frank told us it was a narrow, two-lane road, and was packed when he came through it weeks before, so it was probably too dangerous.

The second route was a road called Old Owen, but it required going across the commercial part of town. Commercial was a synonym for population, which was now a synonym for zombies. So, no go on Old Owen.

Our final bet was a road close to our current location. It was called Lewis Street. There was a bridge, and then a back road called Ben Howard. It ran parallel to Highway 2, but since it was a back road, it wouldn't be too populated. After we crossed the Lewis Street Bridge, there would be one more before we reached Sultan.

"When should we leave?"

Frank looked forlorn. "I'm tired, Cyrus. I'm an old man. Haven't gotten a night's sleep in months now. I'd like to stay until morning."

"Are you two okay with that?"

Gabe and Blaze nodded. Blaze said, "It seems like a good idea, since we don't know about those cars."

Frank pushed up off the sofa. "I'm going to check the kitchen out, ya'll. See if I can get us some food. Hell, I can even warm it up on the stove."

The casualness of our situation was strange. The city was full of undead, but none of them had discovered us here yet. I wondered if that would all change through the night. The living dead had a way of finding you no matter how quiet you were, or how safe you thought you were.

I heard crunching in the kitchen, where I found Pickle chomping on old cat food on the linoleum. The little ferret seemed to be enjoying it well enough, so I didn't stop her.

Blaze tapped my shoulder. I craned my neck around to look at her. "Yeah?"

"Let's clean you up. Your face isn't looking too good."

Oh, yeah. I remembered half my face was scraped by a vicious wall at the prison. Just thinking about it made the wounds hurt.

Fatigued, I got up and followed her into the same master bedroom we just had our tiff in. She sat down at the bottom edge of the bed and shrugged her camouflage jacket off, revealing a white, sleeveless undershirt. Dog tags rested just above the low neckline. Without the bulk of the jacket she had a feminine frame, albeit a lean one.

"Rubbing alcohol should be fine for that," she said, giving a nod toward my face. "Let's check your shoulder, too."

She reached into her backpack and pulled out a brown bottle of rubbing alcohol and some cotton cloths. She sat down next to me and the bed squeaked.

Without care for my discomfort, she loaded one of the cloths with alcohol and got to work on my face. The liquid stung and made my eyes smart. I stared at her neck as she cleaned me up, feeling uncomfortable with the proximity. Her dog tags glinted in the setting sunlight, catching my eye.

Wright, Beatrice.

"Your name is Beatrice?"

"Clearly."

"How did you get the name Blaze?"

Mild surprise crossed her face, as though she never thought about it. "High school, I guess. I was always blazing up. Cigarettes and arson."

"Arson." I winced in pain as she scrubbed a particularly deep gash.

"I was unsatisfied with life."

I chuckled. "Where were you when I was in high school? You'd have been my soul mate."

"Is that so? Take your vest off."

While I unzipped my tactical vest, I stole a quick look at her. She tossed the bloodied cloths on the floor and got some new ones from her pack, followed by a dark glass bottle. It looked like iodine. I hoped it wasn't.

It was unnecessary, but I had the urge to impress the indifferent woman by my side. I pulled my stained undershirt off and turned my bad shoulder to her. She scanned my body in a single, calculated glance.

If she liked the way I looked, she wasn't going to say so. Naturally I was a bit hurt. I wasn't a flabby couch potato. In fact, my time alone in the apartment was so full of sit-ups and push-ups my body was, as the kids say, 'smokin.' I thought so, at least. Unfazed, she tugged off the old bandage and tossed it with the soiled rags. I knew what came next.

"Don't want this to get infected." She uncapped the iodine and saturated a clean cloth with it. "You could lose your arm. Wouldn't want that. This already looks bad."

She pressed the cloth to the cut on my shoulder, and I hissed in pain. Iodine, pure iodine. It hurt more than the wound. Blackness crept into the fringes of my vision.

"Man up."

How would she like it if I aggressively applied iodine to her?

After she was done, she slapped on a new bandage from her endless supply of medical materials, then unlaced her boots. I did the same, eager to free myself from their unforgiving constraint. Plus it gave me something else to focus on, besides the brutal agony in my shoulder.

Frank showed up in the doorway, a pot in one hand. He beamed a gap-toothed grin at us.

"I made soup. Ya'll come eat, now."

I forced myself to get up, put a shirt on, and found that Frank had pulled bowls out and everything. He poured a heavy serving of Chef Boyardee pasta into our bowls then shoved them toward us. Eating hot canned goods was even more bizarre than living in a random house, but I wasn't complaining. I liked Chef Boyardee, and downtime was good, too.

We ate on the sofa, since the dining room was close to a sliding glass door that didn't have blinds. If one zombie saw us, hundreds more would follow his lead and try to break in to eat us.

The meat-stuffed ravioli in tomato sauce tasted better than anything I'd had in quite a while. It used to be a quintessential staple in my apartment before I noticed how fat I was getting from it. Eating it reminded me of better times, and a little bell of sadness rang in my heart.

Despite everything, with my clean wounds and filled belly, I felt like a million bucks. After we ate, we decided to sleep, since the stars were aligned in regard to our safety.

"You girls can sleep in the main bed. I'll take that guest room. Cyrus'll take the couch, all right?"

Gabe's mouth dropped open and she snorted. "I don't think so. I'll take the guest room. No arguments. I'm feeling..."

She swayed slightly and brought her hand up to her head. Without another word, she stumbled into the room with the small bed, shutting it behind her.

"I'll take the couch," Frank said, smiling at Blaze and me.

Without a word, Blaze turned and went to the room. Was Frank trying to set us up? If so, I thought it was a noble attempt at trying to get me laid. After so many years, he was still looking after me.

I followed her in and shut the door. My toes felt remarkable in the carpet as I walked to the bed. Every fiber massaged them, making them feel renewed. I rolled my neck around, cracking it a few times, then laid down. It was blazing (pun intended) in the room, so there was no need for any covers.

As I settled into bed, I exhaled in pleasure. My face and shoulder stung pleasantly from the sanitization, and the bed felt unbelievable.

Blaze lay down next to me on her side, facing away. Her breathing was shallow. I watched from the corner of my eye as her side rose and fell.

Somewhere in the house, the air conditioner whirred to life, its automatic timing uninterrupted by the end of the world. Our good fortune almost made me sing out loud. We were lucky with the house. No runners or slows had found us, but by morning I'd bet there'd be a few. We had food, guns, ammo, two cars, and a plan. My pulse sped up as adrenaline released in my bloodstream.

Calm down, I chided myself. *Just take it easy.*

Breathing deeper, I relaxed once again and forgot about my woes.

A burning orange sunset passed through the beige curtains, illuminating the room. I pictured the sun outside setting across the city like it always had and always would. Some things never changed.

Turning on my good shoulder, I let a tiny sigh escape me. I always was a side sleeper. Until I fell asleep, I watched the last sunlight disappear from the room. I don't know how long I slept. It was strange falling asleep in a lit room and waking up in a black-blue one.

Blaze was on her back, the silhouette of her face washed in the glow of an adjacent alarm clock. It was odd having power on so sporadically. I wondered if the town we were headed for, Sultan, also had that going on. It might make things easier for us.

If Blaze hadn't spoken, I would've thought she was asleep. Somehow she knew I was awake.

"Are you attracted to me?"

"Uh..."

Was I? Sure, kind of. Now that I thought about it, I was. My reactions to Blaze were primarily respect, a little fear, and awe. Since I rarely felt those emotions toward anyone, it made sense for the word "attracted" to explain it all.

Unexpected embarrassment filled me. Even though she probably couldn't see my face, which was contorted in shame, I turned onto my back again. Saving people, making right choices, and now this? Attraction to a female?

Maybe I wasn't as asexual as I thought. Either way, attraction toward her would only confuse things. Plus, it would make Gabe go even more loco. She already hated Blaze Wright with a passion. Whatever the hell was going on here would just fuel the fire.

If someone asked me six months ago if I could see myself in a love triangle, I would have said they were crazy. But was that what I was in? A love triangle? I felt something for Blaze, while she wanted to kill Gabe. Gabe needed me and I protected her, but at the same time I hated her. Geometry wasn't my strong suit, but there was a triangle in there somewhere.

I felt something for Blaze, but was it attraction?

I shot for a cryptic air and said, "Apocalypses do this kind of thing to you."

Bless her soul, all she said was, "They sure do."

Chapter 15

He's weak, Blaze thought as she watched Cyrus sleep. *He can't do what has to be done.*

Someone had to do something about that girl, and it had to be Blaze. That useless, stereotypical father figure wouldn't speak harshly about Gabe, let alone kill her, and Cyrus was no better. Behind his well developed façade was a doubtful, confused man.

But Blaze? No one could make a decision as fast or as practical as she, which was why she was going to take action.

When Cyrus's breath grew even and deep she slid off the bed, careful not to disturb him, and carried her pack into the bathroom. After the door clicked shut she held her breath and listened, but heard nothing.

Entering a hospital was an obvious death sentence, but Blaze was glad she had. If she hadn't gone to find Carolyn, she wouldn't have the sedative and needle needed to get rid of Gabe.

She went through the process of filling the hypodermic needle with a sedative, going through the motions as she'd seen in the movies. Draw the liquid up, tap the needle, squirt a little out. Blaze clenched the needle in her hand and took a breath.

Killing Gabe was too easy. If she wanted to, she could walk into her room and slit her throat or suffocate her, but that wasn't enough. Blaze hated the girl, so she wanted her to suffer.

The house was quiet, save for the old man on the living room couch. Frank was snoring loud enough to wake the dead. She snickered at her joke as she walked by him. If their location was compromised, it would be because of him.

No noise came from Gabe's room, but a subdued white light shone from underneath the door. The girl's stupidity knew no bounds; a light was a beacon for the undead.

She turned the knob slowly, pleased that it wasn't locked. Inside, Gabe was lying on her back on a twin mattress. A flashlight was on the ground with a pillowcase over it. The only window was covered with heavy tacky drapes, which was why Gabe must've left her makeshift nightlight on. Blaze doubted it was visible from the outside, but she'd never risk such a thing.

Blaze stepped into the room and shut the door behind her, needle in hand. The door shut quietly, but once she was looming over her sleeping figure, the girl's eyes opened.

"What are you—"

She pressed her hand over Gabe's mouth and brought her knee onto the bed, immobilizing her arm. Gabe tried to use her free hand to push Blaze's hand off her mouth, but Blaze easily overpowered her.

Blaze injected the sedative into her squirming arm and continued holding her down. Gabe was small and malnourished. The sedative worked faster than she expected it to, and the struggling girl's eyelids fluttered and her body went limp.

Everything was running according to plan. No noise indicated she'd woken anyone up or drawn attention from the undead outside. To be sure, Blaze waited until she was confident before continuing her plan.

In the morning when they discovered Gabe was gone, they'd look in her room—of course—and there could be no evidence of a struggle or any of her items left behind. From her boots to her backpack and coat, Blaze stashed them in the room's small chest of drawers. Although she didn't think Cyrus or Frank would go as far as to search the room, she made sure to place clothes atop everything. Gabe's pack was too large for the drawers so she shoved it under the bed and tugged the bed skirt down. Blaze hadn't brought a gun or flashlight of her own because she planned on taking Gabe's.

Once she was done and had the gun slung over her shoulder, the only sign of Gabe was Gabe herself, her breath shallow and her body motionless. Blaze tested her level of sedation by shaking her and was pleased with the results. She picked her up and positioned her over her shoulder, glad Gabe was small and light.

Blaze was strong and healthy up until the prison. After a week of barely existent rations and water, she wasn't feeling too hot herself.

When they arrived at the house, she noted a garden shed in the backyard, which was where Gabe was headed. The fastest route was through the sliding glass door, and the blinds would make a lot of noise when she raised them. However, the front door and garage would make noise as well.

Blaze opted for raising the blinds. She did so slowly, wincing at each squeak. Frank's snoring never faltered, even as she clicked the lock up and slid the door open just enough to squeeze through.

Outside seemed more dead than usual. Above, the night sky was clear and the weather cold. The lack of tall trees surrounding the house allowed for the moon to provide just enough light to see. The fresh air was still tinged with the faint sent of rot, despite the soft breeze blowing around the house. No undead were in sight. Even if they were in a neighbor's yard, they wouldn't see Blaze. There was no fencing leading into the backyard from the front, but walls of overgrown evergreen shrubs flanked both sides in the back. They were just tall enough to grant cover.

Blaze propped the girl against the shed and gripped the MP5. The shed was unassuming, but it was just the place for someone to hide a dying—or already dead—loved one. She jerked the door open and stepped back behind it simultaneously, waiting for a sign of an undead.

Nothing came out and there was no noise. She withdrew Gabe's flashlight and leaned around the door, shining it in only briefly to confirm there was nothing inside. She then picked Gabe up and set her on the shed floor next to a lawn mower.

It was only a few hours until dawn, and that's when they'd be leaving. The bottle's label said the recommended dose for a patient's age and bodyweight would keep them under for at least four hours. Blaze used more than Gabe needed, but not more than she thought was safe.

That was the point, after all. To make sure Gabe stayed alive. She brought her to the shed to abandon her, leaving her with nothing. When she woke up, they'd be long gone and she'd be completely alone. For her, that would be more of a punishment than death. She'd have to find someone again, but this time she wouldn't be as lucky. No shoes, no gun, no clue of where she was.

Blaze's shoulder felt light as she shut the door and walked back to the house, and it wasn't just because Gabe wasn't on it.

Chapter 16

Smoke snaked around the ceiling, looking down at me with mild interest. It was thick up there and made intricate swirling patterns as air moved through it. My lungs felt a little singed. Why didn't I wake up sooner?

Another question made its way through my groggy, sleep-addled brain. How could Blaze smoke that many cigarettes? That amount of smoke was more like the house being on fire, not...

Oh.

To my side, Blaze slept on her stomach. Her head was turned to the side, and I saw a glimmer of drool run off onto the pillow. There wasn't a cigarette in sight, but I could smell ash as she exhaled.

The house is on fire.

"The house is on fire!"

I flung myself out of bed, knocking my head on the nightstand. A brief show of stars swirled around me before I was up and yanking on my boots.

Blaze was in motion, both of her shoes on and tied before I got to my second one. I grabbed my vest and pack, pulling them on hastily, then grabbed my rifle. Words already on my lips, I turned to Blaze to tell her to hurry up, but she stood there as though she lived to be ready for anything.

"Calm down." She grabbed my arm as I went to throw open the door. "We can't run out there without knowing the situation."

"If you open the window they'll see us!"

"Would you rather just run out?" she hissed. "One way or another we *have* to see what's out there. There might be more guarding out front, and if we walk out there we'll be shot."

She went to the blinds before I could disagree any further and pulled them aside, just a tad, to reveal the backyard. I came up beside her and looked.

Dozens of living, armed people were out there.

The Hummer was pried open and someone worked on hotwiring it. They were going to steal it and everything inside. Every gun and bullet we had been taking for granted would be gone.

A shout caught our attention. Some guy in motorcycle garb pointed at us, waving some kind of machine gun wildly in the other hand.

Chances of us stopping that many people? Slim. Chances of us getting shot? Burned to death? Eaten alive? Left for dead? Very, very high.

"Well, looks like we're royally fucked." Blaze gritted her teeth.

"What're we going to do?"

"Fucking kill them."

A grim expression shrouded her face as she dropped the blinds back. Only a moment later, shards of glass cascaded onto us as we hit the floor and crawled to the only exit in the room. Now that the window was out, we could hear the bastards outside even better. They wanted to kill us. No surprise there.

When we made it to the door, Blaze reached up and unlocked it, jerking it open. We crawled through and took cover behind the wall before moving up into a crouch.

Frank was already by the garage entrance, pressed up against the wall. He glanced at the two of us then across the living room to the guestroom door where Gabe was.

"I'll get the other girlie. We gotta get out of here!"

Another burst of gunfire in the bedroom.

He was just about to make a dash down the hall when Blaze grabbed him by the shoulder roughly.

"She's gone. She left last night."

Frank's mouth dropped open and my eyebrows rose in surprise. Gabe left? On her own? That defied her need to be taken care of. I wasn't about to take Blaze's word for it. Not after she'd expressed a desire to take Gabe out.

"How the fuck do you know?"

"There's no time to talk about this, Cyrus!"

Without explaining myself, I moved low and quickly to Gabe's room. The door was open, which made sense if Gabe left in the night.

She was gone. The bed looked slept in. Her belongings were nowhere to be seen. It didn't make sense, but Blaze hadn't been lying about her being gone. Whether it was because of Blaze or not that Gabe left, I didn't have time to think about.

Glass shattered somewhere in the house. Moans of the undead joined the symphony of yells outside, and so did the frantic shouting of the thieves. Frank produced a bottle of rum and shoved a dirty rag into it.

"Where the hell did you get that?" Blaze said.

"I found it."

"Of course," I said, clenching my rifle a little harder.

"We can't lose that Hummer," Blaze said. "It'd be an unforgivable setback. If we can run out and manage to get into the Hummer, we can just drive away from all this. Let's go out the front and loop around."

"There's about ten of them out there," Frank said. "Our luck is just as good taking them head on."

Blaze and I agreed. We moved down the hallway and into the living room. The sliding glass door leading to the backyard was destroyed. A woman leaned around the corner, getting ready to enter. She was jerked out of sight, followed by a piercing scream. For a moment she reappeared, but fell face first to the ground. As she tried to get up and crawl away, her body was pulled backward. Most of her chin and lower lip was ripped off and blood gushed from the wounds.

Blaze motioned for Frank and me to move forward. I assumed she was going to cover us. I took the left side of the opening and Frank took the right. From my new point, I could see the group outside being overrun by zombies. So far the living were winning, but once we joined the battle the tides would turn.

The woman's body was gone. I saw her wriggling body being eaten alive by two slows. They were too engrossed to notice a man come up behind them and put a bullet in their heads. The man didn't notice me as he dropped to his knees, sobbing over the woman.

I forced my attention away from him. He wasn't a threat. Our Hummer was close, but it seemed painfully far away when there was a battle between us and it. It was time to take chances and ignore the danger. That Hummer was basically my livelihood. I wasn't letting it go.

The man still worked on hotwiring it. His whole body shook visibly from the stress of chaos and a deadline. Centering his head in my iron sight was too easy. A single bullet went into the back of his head, and he slumped briefly before sliding out of the car.. My gunfire was masked by the rest.

Frank lit his cocktail and threw it near the biggest group of people, both living and dead. The glass broke and the fire spread quickly onto motorcycles and people. More screeches filled the air as the fire consumed everything in its radius.

Blaze came up and went prone in front of me, firing single shots with amazing precision. Not all of her shots hit heads, but she was killing or incapacitating people with righteous fury. From the corner of my eye, I saw her muzzle flash and the dead fell permanently, or the living join them.

"Let's move!" I shouted once a path to the Hummer was visible.

Crackling bodies accompanied by the now familiar scent of burnt human assaulted me. Bodies dropped where Frank threw the cocktail, the wind carrying their putrid scent toward us.

Breathing through my mouth, I ran out first, making a B-line to the vehicle. However, my B-line fell apart when someone knocked me sideways into the slimy, green pool I'd been trying to avoid. Not enough time for me to grab a gulp of air, I ended up taking in a mouthful of earthy, thick water as I plunged in. Bubbles surrounded me and I couldn't see. The chaos above water was muffled, sounded far away. Morning light filtered through the algae-laden water, putting me in a strange world of green.

This is fucking Washington! Who the hell had a below ground swimming pool here? It rained 256 days of the year, for Pete's sake! On the off chance I found the blasted owners of it, I was going to put a bullet in their heads right then.

A tight grip found my ankle and dragged me down farther, pulling me to the deep end. I kicked, but it felt sluggish and ineffective under water. The heel of my boot brushed against something round, and I assumed it was a skull. I kicked again and the hand released.

Need air. Need air.

My rifle was gone, making it easier to struggle to the surface. Once my head broke the waterline, I took in a ragged breath. I'd been struggling for only a few minutes, but another dozen undead had appeared out of nowhere, eagerly trying to snag brunch.

I glanced down just in time to see a dark shape move under me and grab both my legs. This time I managed to take a breath before I was jerked back under. Taking the risk, I reached into my boot to pull out my utility knife. The zombie tried taking a chunk out of my covered foot. I felt it even through the dense boot, two rows of hard teeth.

Knife freed, I ground it into the top of his head. Blood spread out from the wound, clouding the water. I pulled out the knife and pushed from the bottom of the pool to the surface again.

No enemies congested one side of the pool, so I swam to that vicinity as fast as my sopping wet clothing would allow. Just as I was pulling myself up, a hand grabbed at my leg. Blaze showed up and caught me by the vest just as I was about to go back under. Through the water in my eyes, I saw a figure sprinting toward her.

Effortlessly, she let go of me, spinning around. She took the butt of her rifle to the head of a runner intent on taking advantage of her vulnerable position. It fell and she finished the job with another furious smash to its skull.

Blaze moved toward the Hummer and I followed her, wondering where Frank was. The fire pushed the living closer together near the Hummer, which wasn't good for us. They took note of us as we got closer, gesturing and shouting. A few opened fire and I grabbed Blaze, pulling her into the cover of an abandoned blue Mazda. How the hell did they fit this many cars into the backyard?

A familiar, loud engine roared to life.

"Fuck."

Blaze's face drew into a tight grimace. I peered over the car to see the Hummer, our Hummer, crunching over dead bodies as it drove around the house. The hijackers and their team followed, shooting the trailing undead.

Some of the men and women were getting on their motorcycles and in their cars, speeding up their exit.

"Fuck!" Blaze shouted.

Frank showed up, breathless. His mouth and nose were bleeding, but other than that he was his usual self.

"We gotta get outta here. Every flesh eater in a ten mile radius must've heard the commotion!"

Where were we going to go? And how? I remembered the Mustang and saw it wasn't stolen. Well, that was great. We had a useless sports car that paled in comparison to the behemoth of a Hummer.

Moans and groans caught my ear. Just because the living were gone didn't mean we were in the clear. Zombies came from everywhere. Dead bodies twitched, getting ready to come back.

"Okay," I said as I scrambled to my feet. "Gather up all the guns and whatever supplies are around. Put them in the Mustang. Let's go."

Blaze and Frank nodded then rushed about, grabbing all manner of weapons left behind. I dodged a decrepit zombie wriggling on the ground as I picked up an old shotgun.

As the minutes passed by, at least ten people would come back from the dead. The thought of ten runners was horrifying, even to me.

After opening the Mustang door, I shoved an armful of guns into the backseat. Probably not the safest way, just dropping them, but I was bending time as it was. Frank and Blaze did the same, then Blaze slid into the backseat.

"There's still more stuff," I scolded, but was reprimanded by Frank.

"Boy, I don't think you're aware, but there's a hell of a lot of zombies coming our way."

My focus went from him to said stiffs shambling toward us. They were only yards away and closing in fast. Some of the bodies on the ground were twitching. A sure sign they would be rising soon.

"Right, right." I settled myself into the driver's seat.

Once we were all secure, I hit the gas and we left the backyard. My heart thumped wildly and I felt extremely disgruntled. All my clothes, my backpack, and Pickle…

Pickle!

I slammed on the brakes and shimmied out of my pack, then almost stuck the zipper as I yanked it open. A wet, pissed off ferret flew out and headed into the backseat. Water leaked through the zippers, but the rest of the fabric prevented her from drowning.

Blaze and Frank were staring at me. I returned the look indifferently.

"She means a lot to me."

We were off.

* * *

Don't get me wrong, I liked planning, and certainly wouldn't bitch about doing it. However, when my plan was compromised…well, that's a different story.

Compromise was not having everything you brought from home. Compromise was driving a little car. Compromise was being soaking wet and slimy.

My mind went to how Gabe just up and left. Maybe I was just wallowing in the loss of the Hummer and wanted to pile the bad things up, just to make the wallowing a little more pitiful. But Gabe was on her own now, and didn't need the help of one Cyrus V. Sinclair anymore. Rumor had it that no one needed his help anymore.

"We might want to find a store and get food. Maybe loot a gun shop," Blaze said, breaking me from my destructive thoughts. "Since we're raped of all our supplies."

I shook my head. "We'll find food, maybe, but there's no way a store with any firepower isn't already looted or decimated in some way. Gas stations are one thing, but a gun shop is another. It's pointless. I can't believe you even suggested that."

Blaze's face darkened. "Don't test me, Cyrus. We're all angry right now, but that doesn't mean we're going to be bitches in heat over it."

"Sorry," I grumbled, mentally blocking her out.

I checked the rearview mirror. A small group of Zs stumbled along after us. Ahead, a house to my right had a sheet hanging from two second story windows. In ragged, blue letters it stated alive inside.

I doubted that.

"We could go after them. Get the Hummer back," I said, but discarded the idea. We didn't leave soon enough to catch which direction they went. It was a 50/50 chance (right or left) but if we chose incorrectly, it would be a futile chase for nothing.

"Yeah, great idea, captain. We certainly showed them who was boss," Blaze said.

Frank rubbed his hand along his grey, stubbly beard and laughed. "Ya'll are overreactin'."

Blaze huffed loudly from the back. She didn't think we were overreactin'. Neither did I.

"No," he continued, "really. You didn't always have that Hummer. What happened was ya'll got cocky and dependent on it. Ya'll were actin' like it was your momma and you couldn't do a damn thing without 'er."

There was truth in Frank's words. Maybe I was being a tad melodramatic about the whole thing. Blaze too. Losing everything just made the adventure more challenging. And what was life without a challenge? We'd lost sight of that with all of our excessiveness.

Blaze admitted, "He's right."

The corner of my mouth twitched into a smirk. If she could admit she was being foolish, so could I.

"I suppose we should continue on with our plan. Go to the bridge. Keep heading to Frank's cabin."

Francis and Blaze voiced agreement. Getting to the Lewis Street bridge would be easy enough, and I had committed the rest of the route to memory from the maps. If the roads weren't too clogged, it would only take ten minutes to arrive at Sultan. We had to cross another bridge leading into Sultan, at 311th Ave, but after that we only needed to follow Highway 2 to the end of the next town, where the Kellogg Lake Road entrance was located. The drive and hike required to reach the cabin was lengthy, but wasn't populated.

Older houses with overgrown lawns sat lost and forgotten, looking eerie in the bright sunlight. Some had shattered windows and broken doors, while others simply looked as though the owners left. Or were they still inside? I didn't doubt some of them were, dead or maybe even alive.

I turned the car left and passed a white minivan. A group of kids turned their heads and followed the Mustang as we passed, clawing at us through closed windows. Up in the front seat, a set of parents struggled against their seatbelts. Kind of funny, really. A genuine zombie family with a mommy, daddy, and two kids.

Seeing the people in the van made me wonder about all the Zs who were stuck in a situation like that. They were too stupid to open doors normally, or unbuckle seatbelts. Hypothetically, if someone tried to get the world back together, how long would it take? How much effort would it take to clear out every house, car, tent, cabin, RV—every location people went to hide. Probably forever.

Even if we thought the job was complete and we were living in zombie-free peace for years, all it would take was one bite and a dose of stupidity to start the cycle again. A part of me hoped that new world would learn from our mistakes, but I doubted it.

"Take a left," Frank said.

I turned left, glad that he mentioned it. I'd almost forgotten. Houses on this street were burned up into charred, black skeletons. Tuning out the destruction, and any other thoughts, I just drove.

When we approached the bridge, I stopped. There were bodies hanging from the support beams.

Chapter 17

That's rather disturbing, I thought, as we approached the bridge entrance.

What wasn't disturbing, in any way, were the sandbags blocking our path. Good luck was temporary luck, so I wasn't too displeased. Beyond the sandbags was a fairly clear stretch of road, void of zombies or other hindrances.

Corpses dangled above, jiggling and stretching their grey arms down toward us. I wondered why they were up there, and if they'd gone willingly or were strung up by force or after they died. Either way, a good twenty of them writhed foolishly, thinking they had a shot at getting us. Some were high up, others almost touched the ground.

Stifling a groan, I stopped the car, my knuckles going white as I clenched the steering wheel. Since the dead started coming back, I had seen a lot of things. Destroyed corpses walking around outside my apartment, people eating and destroying one another for no reason. Yet each time something alarming occurred, I had to stop and ask myself why? Who in the world thought it would be a good idea to do that?

"If it ain't one thing, it's another," Frank grumbled as he glanced out the window. Deeming the coast clear, he exited the car and approached the barrier.

Blaze and I followed, snatching up our guns before we left. Frank already picked up bags and tossed them off to the side. I could tell he strained to pick up each one.

"Let's get this done quick before he throws his back out," I whispered to Blaze before we were in earshot of Frank.

"That's the least of our worries," she said and nodded toward the hanging zombies.

Now I was out of the car, I could hear their rabid yells along with the rushing of the river. Any undead in range would hear them and come and check things out.

Nonchalance cast aside, I jogged up to Frank and started hauling bags. Blaze took the ones I picked up then handed them to Frank, expediting the process greatly. There were still a lot of bags. The unsettling environment got on my nerves.

A couple yards away, a woman in a ruined set of scrubs gathered momentum, swaying back and forth. She was nowhere near touching me, but every time she got a bit closer I got more nervous.

Gunshots echoed from somewhere. We all paused and listened, but no more ensued.

"You're upset she's gone," Blaze said.

"How did you find the time to deduce that between us finding out Gabe left and us nearly getting killed?"

I shoved the bag at her and she stumbled back a step from my aggression. Blaze smirked, the scar on her right cheek crinkling up. She turned and gave the bag to Frank. I guess my actions spoke louder than words, because she took that as confirmation.

"You're not as perceptive as you think, Wright."

"You're so wrapped up in your image. Seems to me you're pushing yourself to be like this. If you're upset about the kid, don't get defensive about it."

Snorting in outrage, I said, "Yeah? I'm sure you would if you were me. Being attacked."

"I'm not attacking you. And I wouldn't be upset." She stopped in front of me, leaning in close. "The difference between you and I is I don't have to try and be cynical or impassive."

She turned away, passing a bag to Frank, who wore a grin. Apparently he liked it when someone told me off.

"If Frank wasn't here, I'd beat the hell out of you," I said, too low for said man to hear.

Blaze stared at me, her eyebrows raised and her dark eyes wide. "Would you, now?"

"I don't handle psychological probing well."

"Is that what I was doing? Psychologically probing?"

"It's as good a term as any." I thrust a sandbag in her arms.

This time she held her ground, not budging an inch. She was tall and strong, which I had forgotten about. Recollection of her schooling Gabe flooded back to me. Blaze had taken care of that efficiently.

"I'm going to let you cool off, but if you try to fuck around with me, I will reciprocate," she said.

Saying another word would not be wise. Ceasing my childish behavior, I stopped the shoving and bickering and got down to what was important: clearing a path so we could get the hell out of Monroe.

* * *

The opening we created was just big enough for the Mustang to shimmy through. I tried maneuvering around the woman in scrubs, but her hands slid along the side of the car, squelching as skin sloughed off onto the windows.

No one spoke. Troubled by my confrontation with Blaze, I didn't want to make matters worse by talking. Blaze didn't speak unless necessary. And Frank? He'd seen our tiff earlier and probably didn't want to get involved.

Up the bridge a bit, a jumble of unidentifiable wreckage was in the way, but I steered around it without any difficulty.

The bridge was short. We made it across in a few seconds, my thoughts of it ceasing once it was out of sight. I took a left onto Ben Howard Road and saw a blissfully empty stretch of pavement. Not a thing marred it: no zombies, no cars, death, or wreckage. It felt like the three of us were just going on a nice drive through the country.

Blaze rifled through the guns in the backseat, the heavy metal of them clunking loudly. I threw a quick glance back to see what she was doing.

As though she read my mind, she said, "Checking our inventory."

Pickle scurried up my leg and settled into my lap. I stroked her fur, admiring how resilient the ferret was through all of this. Being kidnapped by bigots, almost drowning—she had a lot of close calls recently, but was putting her best paw forward, every time.

The clicking and sliding of Blaze's inspection stopped. "You lost your carbine, correct?"

"Yeah, back at the pool. I have my .40 and my 9mm."

"Lucky for you, I picked one up. If you have ammo in your pack, I suggest taking this. I've consolidated another four clips for you. Frank, you still have your rifle and ammo. I've got some rounds for you, too."

Feelings about the Hummer tried to wiggle their way back into my brain, but I forced it all away. We wouldn't even need that much ammunition to get to the cabin. The excess was fortunate, but not necessary. Hell, I even had a replacement carbine.

I really needed to be grateful for the little things.

The Mustang handled the curvy back road easily. The entire time we only saw a few zombies, who didn't even look dead. Just a bite here or there must've turned them. Except for their pallid skin and cloudy eyes, they could've passed for the living.

My stomach rumbled, breaking the white noise of the engine and my mundane thoughts. I hadn't eaten since last night, and before that I'd only eaten some junk in the convenience store. Too bad most of the MREs were gone.

There was at least one left in my pack, but I wasn't sure if the others had food.

Thinking about food made me even hungrier. A painful craving for sweetened condensed milk, Pop Rocks, and Snickers bars swept over me. Despite my constant wishful thinking, sweets were priority two, compared to actual sustenance that contained protein, fiber, and carbohydrates.

"What about the food situation?"

Blaze rummaged through all our packs for a couple minutes and came up with the one MRE, some gummy bears, a protein bar, and a few bottles of water. The MRE was spaghetti with meat sauce. Appetizing.

I stopped the car, leaving it idling, and reached back for the MRE. We decided to each take a third of it and share one bottle of water. It would have to do until we found somewhere to raid, or got lucky. Heaven knew luck hadn't graced us with her presence recently. She was long, long overdue.

No one wanted the gummy bears, so I took those for myself.

The spaghetti was edible, but not enjoyable. While in the midst of an apocalypse, a guy couldn't care about flavor. Like a man, I swallowed my portion in gulps before passing it to Frank, who took more time. All that man ever ate was MREs, so I figured it wasn't an issue for him.

A slimy, artificial tomato taste coated every surface in my mouth. I ran my tongue over my teeth repeatedly, hoping to rid myself of it. In that moment, I'd easily consider killing Blaze and giving up my first born (not like I'd ever have one) for a toothbrush or bottle of Listerine. Poor hygiene and a lack of firepower weighed heavily on my morale. Feeling dirty, itchy, and unprepared grouped me with the rest of the survivors. I hated that.

Ahead and to my left, the brush on the side of the road stirred. A man in a sheriff's outfit fell out and onto the ground. Not a heartbeat later, he got to his feet and dragged himself toward us. There was a gaping hole where his stomach used to be, ragged ends of intestines slipping out.

"Time to go," I said and put the car back into drive.

Our happy lunch over, we set off again.

The sheriff lunged toward the Mustang as we passed, and fell yet again to the hard asphalt. I watched in the rearview mirror as he disappeared behind us.

"We have to think about when and where we'll stop for supplies," I said, even though trying to drive straight through sounded appealing. "I know your cabin is stocked, but as we all know, things don't go according to plan. It might take multiple days to get there. I don't want to be starving to death during that time."

Two towns and a lot of road stood between us and the cabin. While it should take twenty minutes to pass through, considering how long it took to get through Monroe, it was feasible Sultan or the next town, Startup, might slow us down. We still had to hike a ways into the mountains, and we'd need food then.

Frank said, "Depending on how Sultan is, we can look there. We'll enter about a mile from the town grocery store."

"I don't like the idea of backtracking," Blaze said. "If we see any houses along this road, why don't we check them out? They're bound to have canned goods in them, if anything."

I agreed, and began to verbalize, but Frank cut me off. "The people out here know how to defend themselves. The houses out here, well, they're probably all boarded up."

"We can still try, Frank. Better to take chances out here than inside an infested town," Blaze countered, an edge of impatience in her voice.

On occasion, she was easy to read. Her story about where she was when hell broke loose showed her lack of concern toward family or children. Now her general attitude toward Frank showed her great impatience for the elderly. It gave me the impression that Blaze was all about efficiency and everyone being on board for The Plan, no matter what it was.

"It's true," I agreed. "If we get lucky out here, we wouldn't have to worry about it again. We just need enough to last us until we get to the cabin, right?"

He chewed on his lip, and then nodded slowly. "Yeah, I guess ya'll are right. Just be wary, 'cause some strange people live in these woods."

The discussion ended and we lapsed into silence once more. A pungent, unmistakable scent wafted into my nostrils. Blaze lit up a cigarette. Frank pawned one off her and they both smoked up the car. I rolled the window down and let the hot summer air carry the smoke away.

Sounds of the river and wind whipping through trees were quintessential to the season. When the apocalypse started, it was a very rainy and fitting April. Time flew by quickly when I was on my own, and even when Gabe was with me in the apartment. Now time crawled. Getting from point A to point B was riddled with quarreling and impediments of all sorts.

When I was a little kid, life was painstakingly slow. Summer seemed like a decade, which made going back to school that much worse. As I grew older, a summer was gone in the blink of an eye. *Every* day came and went like that. I stopped caring when I was a teenager.

Yet normal people hated the passage of time. They hated feeling like their lives were slipping away. Now I'd kill for a day like that. A day where an hour didn't seem like four and every task tripled in difficulty.

Blaze was abnormal, so I wondered how she perceived things. Did she also think time slowed down when the dead walked? What did she think about *anything*? I knew she was callous, and couldn't give a rat's ass about another human, but what about the "whys." Why did the dead start rising? Why did people go crazy so fast? Why did the government fail?

Or the big question; why was she an emotional robot?

I stopped myself from laughing and glanced at the gas gauge. There was only a fourth of the tank left. If we didn't get gas at some point, we were screwed. If we didn't get food, we'd be hungry and screwed. If the house we picked was full of crazies, well, a lot of variables added up to one general concept: We'd be screwed.

"Really strange people," Frank said, having not dropped the subject yet.

With no more time to ponder Blaze's persona, I said, "Three trained and armed professionals versus a few desperate civilians? What's the worst that could happen?"

Chapter 18

Frank knew someone who used to live nearby. He said her name was Judy-Beth, the sister of his Vietnam friend Buggy. In the war, Buggy impressed him with his valuable survival skills. His whole family was taught to be self-sufficient if not antisocial. Frank met Judy-Beth once to deliver the news of Buggy's death. That was close to forty years ago. Since then a distant friend told Frank Judy-Beth died and the house was abandoned. Frank didn't appear to believe the story of her death even as he told it.

"Why didn't you bring this up earlier?" Blaze asked.

"If you couldn't tell, girlie, I'm not keen on stopping anywhere back here. Until you cross the mountains, the farther east you go the crazier everyone gets."

"But she's dead."

"I don't know that for sure," Frank said. "But if she's alive and in that house, there ain't no way she isn't a lunatic."

"Frank, if she's alive she's a frail old woman, and—"

He cut me off. "I'm her age, boy. Do I look frail and old?"

Blaze coughed to mask a laugh.

"No, sir," I said. "But there's no way in hell she could take on the three of us. Even if she has a couple friends, we're better off."

"And if she's alone, or the house is abandoned, we have nothing to worry about," Blaze added to reassure Frank.

He scowled at me before giving Blaze the same face. No one could convince him if his mind was set, and he was set on Judy-Beth being alive and capable of harming one or all of us. We all dropped the subject.

Once we decided to find her house, we found it without issue. Frank's memory was impeccable, even though he'd only been to the house a handful of times. It was an odd shade of blue with peeling paint and junk strewn about its yard. The roof on a poorly built side extension was about to cave in. A black, wicked looking wrought iron fence circled the property. Dense forest shrouded the house, making it look creepier than it had the right to look. If I saw the house pre-apocalypse, I'd call it white trash in a heartbeat. Now it was something from a horror movie.

I drove down a short, gravely road and stopped a couple yards from the front gate. The house didn't need boarding up. Whoever owned it decided to get bars placed over all the windows, even on the second story. Breaking in through a window would be impossible, but that didn't matter. The front door was visible, and had no coverings.

The windows on first-story apartments or bars in Seattle were often barred, but the reason was obvious; it was a big city with a lot of derelicts who had no issue with breaking in. Whenever I saw houses outside of the city with barred windows, I wondered if the owners were keeping something out or in. My morbid side said they were keeping something in.

Something about the place made me feel uncomfortable. Was it the old tricycle on its side in front of the gate? Or the liquid shadows underneath the front porch? How about the curtains in the windows? I could've sworn I saw them shift.

Not letting the spooks get to me, I got out of the car first and reached into the backseat for my new carbine. Blaze handed it to me then slid out, looking at the house with evident suspicion.

Now that I was out of the car, I noted the sullen absence of birds chirping or other expected noises. Of course, this only added to my sense of unease.

"How do you want to do this?"

Maybe Blaze felt wrong about the place, too. Why else would she be whispering?

She spat her cigarette onto the ground and dug her boot into it before looking at me.

"I guess we should just go right in." I shrugged and strolled over to the gate, trying hard for nonchalance.

I heard gravel crunching behind me, and a car door slammed as Frank and Blaze followed. They stopped when I stopped and we all looked at the gate together.

It was locked. A huge, thick chain wrapped around the double gates, padlocked several times over. Nothing could be easy. I threw my gun around my shoulder and grabbed the bars, quickly hoisting myself up. They rattled noisily as I climbed to the top and began my descent to the other side.

After I jumped to the ground, I looked at the two from the other side. "Can you make it, Frank?"

"I'm not totally incapable, boy. I've climbed more fences than you have in your life."

Francis went first, a little slower than me. His boots slipped against the bars, but eventually he made it over. Blaze, as expected, was over in a flash, standing with us and looking at the house again.

Once we were all on the other side, I took another look at the property. The grass was beyond dead, and everything on top of it forgotten and destroyed. Rusted houshold appliances, kids' toys, and other random objects were cluttered together. It looked like the family decided to never throw anything away. Near the side extension, I noticed a mountain of black garbage sacks.

From somewhere behind the house came the faint humming of a generator.

I brought my gun up and walked toward the front door, caution in every step. There was no way I considered the house abandoned. It was too well fortified.

"Fuck!" I yelled as a loud whining noise started up and petered out. My pulse was throbbing in my throat as I looked for its source. A toy truck off to my right. It must've gone off on its own. Its warped, waterlogged sound scared the hell out of me. I glanced at Frank and Blaze, who also looked a bit pale.

Just as I was about to put my boot on the first step up the porch, a muffled voice called out from inside.

"Who are you?" The voice was old and high-pitched. A woman.

I lowered my gun and motioned for my companions to do the same. "My name is Cyrus. This is Frank and Blaze."

"I like those names. Very honorable. What do you want?"

"We're just looking for food. We're hungry," Blaze said in a tone I'd never heard before. I knew the real Blaze, who used one general, flat tone for everything. This voice was higher and subtly mimicking the woman inside. She was quite the actor and psychologist when useful.

"Oh, oh, oh. Well, I can't have that." Clanks of deadbolts being pulled. "Can't have you children going hungry."

A nappy, tall old lady stood in the now open doorway. Her hair was a million shades of grey and stuck up in an equal number of directions. She wore a grossly stained floral skirt and a white blouse. Heavy boots completed the ensemble.

"My name is Judy-Beth. Please come in."

I stole a glance at Frank, who raised his eyebrows at me before proceeding in. Judy-Beth led the way, not looking back once at her guests. Apparently she didn't recognize Frank.

The interior of the house was worse than the outside by a long shot. A narrow walkway guided us through boxes piled up to the ceiling. They had words scribbled in black marker, but I couldn't read any of it. Most of them had water damage or mold growing at their bases, and they smelled musty.. Bare fluorescent light bulbs swung from the ceiling

I wasn't even sure what part of the house we were in. Living room? Dining area? What the fuck was this? Why was the carpet so unevenly brown? It felt like I'd walked into a surreal dimension straight out of the Twilight Zone.

Judy-Beth made a sharp right and Frank followed. Just before Blaze fixed to follow, I grabbed her arm. She moved closer to me and leaned in.

"Something isn't right," I whispered.

Blaze was so close I could see her bloodshot eyes in detail, which were framed with uncommonly long lashes. She blinked and I mentally slapped myself for admiring her.

"I know," she replied, "but don't make any rash decisions."

So far there was nothing apparent to be afraid of, so I didn't feel like making any "rash decisions". All we'd seen was a white-trash house and an old woman. An old woman! We were on edge because we were letting the surroundings get to us. Oddly colored carpet and shadows under the porch…what was I? Six years old?

Unable to help myself, I noticed another strange thing to add to my list. The house smelled positively foul. It smelled like the undead—rotten, musky, and overtly disgusting. Paired with the scent of old house and cardboard, I was overwhelmed. I made the right turn and found myself standing next to a staircase. The scent wafted down the steps and was stronger there.

What did she have up there? Dead bodies? Ah, there I was again. A ludicrous thought process allowed my imagination to go wherever the hell it wanted.

"Excuse me, but please don't dally," came Judy-Beth's voice. Startled, I found her standing right in front of me, teeth bared in a yellow smile. The crevices in her mouth and teeth were browned and decayed. Now that I was up close and personal with her, I noticed how papery and fuzzy her skin was.

As I looked passed her I noticed a kitchen. Blaze and Frank were sitting at its only table. Forcing myself to smile, I squeezed passed her, taking a seat next to Frank.

"You have a mighty fine home here, Judy-Beth," Frank said as he glanced around the kitchen. "You keep a nice house."

The stained and scuffed table stood upon yellowed linoleum tile that looked as though it hadn't been washed in its whole existence. Puke-green paisley wallpaper peeked at me from the edges of cupboards and appliances. Sarcasm dictated I should have said it was a quaint kitchen. Perhaps the only redeeming quality was a bubbling pot on the stove, emitting the rich smell of stew.

Judy-Beth didn't acknowledge Frank's comment, but made her way around the cramped space by the stove, where she stirred whatever was in the pot. We traded looks, but remained silent.

"You're lucky you showed up when you did. I've been cooking this all day," she whispered like she was talking to herself rather than us.

"If you'd rather, we could just take a few canned goods and leave," Frank said.

The snarly woman spun around, waving a spoon at us, and spat. "Don't be foolish! I'm hospitable."

Something was wrong with her. I didn't want to stick around. What I wanted to do was kill her and take whatever we could use in the house. However, that seemed a little too violent and unnecessary, even for me.

Too violent for me, but what about her? Blaze sat across from me and caught me looking at her. Her face remained passive, but I felt as though she knew I was thinking about her. Blaze would kill Judy-Beth. *Did she kill Gabe?*

That idea hit me like a brick. We never talked about what happened to Gabe or how Blaze knew she was gone. Blaze hated her, and Gabe happened to leave in the middle of the night without an explanation? If that wasn't suspicious, I didn't know what was.

There was a thump upstairs and all of us, including Judy-Beth, looked up at the ceiling. She mumbled and turned to the sink, twisting on the faucet.

"You have running water," I said.

"I'm off the grid, you hear? I don't rely on no one." Judy-Beth dropped a plate into the sink. It clanked but didn't break.

After many unbearably quiet minutes, the woman placed cleaned bowls in front of us and ladled stew into each. It looked unremarkable—like any other brownish beef stew I'd ever had in my life.

But it tasted off. Not terrible, but off. It dredged up memories of freezer burn on TV dinners, when I first started living on my own. TV dinners were all I ate then. If I could've replaced the refrigerator with one giant freezer, I would've been a happy camper.

Judy-Beth watched us intently, then lifted the pot and shimmied around the table to the kitchen entrance.

"I'm going to feed my grandchildren. They're sick and can't come down. You, Mr. Cyrus, can get a couple cans of food from the basement."

Before she left, she gestured toward a door adjacent to the refrigerator. I hadn't noticed it before, since it was covered in the same wallpaper as the rest of the kitchen.

"All right. Thank you," I said as I placed my spoon on the table.

We heard the creaking of steps as she made her way upstairs, then nothing. I glanced to the door, then at Blaze and Frank.

Blaze leaned in and whispered, "This stuff tastes nasty. I say we get out of here."

Frank nodded vigorously and motioned to get up.

"No, you stay here. I'm still going downstairs to see what I can get.. I'll be quick," I promised, as I shoved my chair back and stood up.

The two of them sat back in their chairs, looking restless. Their bowls of stew remained untouched.

I hurried to the door and opened it to find a steep, wooden staircase. A coolness washed over me, and I peered into the darkness fleetingly before heading down.

Normally I never got "feelings" or "spooked" or anything like that. Every situation was the same—just a situation—so why get bothered? But this house, in the middle of nowhere, was unpleasant, and I wasn't afraid to admit it.

Windows along the top walls lit the basement, letting in natural light. Down there was the same as upstairs and outside: packed with junk. I maneuvered my way around jumbles of metal objects and boxes until I came to full-wall shelving near a giant freezer.

Crazies always knew how to stock up. Judy-Beth had the shelves lined with canned fruit, vegetables, and meats. It was practically a shopping center. I searched the area for something to put the cans in, and found an old scratchy potato bag. Lately I couldn't afford to be picky, but today I took my time and filled it with my favorites.

Hallelujah! There were a few cans of godly goodness, otherwise known as sweetened condensed milk, behind a stack of peas. I put one in the bag and another in my pants pocket, just in case. It was a tight fit, but it was comforting to have it on my person. The potato sack was bursting at the seams it was so full of sustenance. Carefully, I lifted it from the cement floor and threw it over my shoulder.

The bag broke just as I turned to leave. Cans clunked as the hit the ground and rolled away. Irritated, I crouched down to pick them up, but quickly withdrew my hand. The scowl on my face disappeared. Even through my gloves I felt a slickness coating their exteriors. A can of corn slipped right through my hands as I brought it up to investigate. Instead I concentrated hard on the floor, and once my eyes adjusted to the darker areas, I saw dark splotches circling the freezer where the cans rolled under.

Old blood, I thought. Once I concentrated, I picked up on the coppery scent of it.

My pulse quickened as I rose, eyes fixated on the freezer. There were no noises coming from it, or movement. No threat. Had I been smart, I would've left right then, but I couldn't bring myself to it. Curiosity grabbed hold and wouldn't let go.

I grabbed the edge of the rectangular box and lifted. Cold air slithered out and down the freezer's metal sides. A frost-burned meat scent assaulted me as I opened the lid fully.

A dead man resided inside. Ice crystals covered him entirely, filling in his old wrinkles and thickening his hair. He was crammed in with his knees drawn close to his chest and his arm around them, a pained look on his face. There was a hammer sticking out of his forehead.

"Oh."

And chunks of his arm had been filleted off. The butcher knife still rested in the bottom of the freezer.

Canned food forgotten, I rushed upstairs, feeling nauseated.

I'd never eaten human stew before. I guess there's a first time for everything.

* * *

"She's got little kids up there. Fucking dead ones."

Before I even got the chance to speak, Blaze was right next to me, mouth up against my ear. Frank was still at the table, looking sallow and ready to go. Blaze's chest rose and fell rapidly.

"What?" was my stupid response.

"Her grandchildren are undead, Sinclair. We need to get the hell out of here!"

"How do you know? Did you go up?"

"I was curious. This whole situation is screwed up. I couldn't help myself. They're chained up. She's trying to feed them that stew."

I didn't need to ask further questions, such as how Blaze got up there unnoticed or why she felt the need to go check things out to begin with. I would've done the same thing.

Frank looked at my empty hands. "Where's the food?"

My stomach lurched. The human in my intestines wasn't sitting well anymore. I shook my head, unwilling to tell them what was in the culinary delight served to us.

"Let's go."

Somewhere upstairs, a floor creaked loudly. I slid my .40 out of its holster and took point quickly, moving back through the box maze. The smell from the staircase, which I now identified as rotting human flesh, seemed even stronger the second time around. We took a left and beheld the front door. Our escape.

"Where are you all going?"

I spun around and found Judy-Beth staring at us, pot of foulness in her hands. She had a mean scowl on her lips and a wicked glint in her eyes. There was a dark, smeared handprint on her blouse that wasn't there before.

"Thank you for your hospitality," Blaze said first, since she was closest to the lunatic, "but we realized we need to get going."

Judy-Beth turned and set the horrendous pot atop a high stack of boxes. "You don't know what hospitality is, you fucking dyke!"

I'd backed up to the front door and reached behind me to turn the knob. I didn't bother checking my back, which was a terrible decision, but I wasn't sure what else to do. Stone still, I pointed my gun at Judy-Beth, waiting for someone to make a move.

She made her move first. I didn't know an old lady could move so fast, but she did. Judy-Beth snatched up a double-barrel shotgun from the depths of junk littered around us and shot.

I put a bullet in her right shoulder, knocking her back and into a pile of boxes. They descended on top of her, which eliciting a long screech from her. One shot wasn't enough for that crazy bitch. Aiming in the general area of her torso, I pulled the trigger four more times until no more noises came from under the landslide of crap. I had to know she was dead; after pulled a few boxes off her, I pointed at her head and unloaded the rest of my clip.

The rage that overtook me was powerful, but I had to come back down to earth. Shaking my bloodlust off, I regained focus and saw Frank leaning against Blaze for support. Blood stained his army-green pants near the left thigh. His face was contorted in pain.

"Buckshot! I'm hurtin' bad."

"Go, just go!" I shouted, motioning for them to pass me.

The moment Blaze and Bordeaux passed me, I slammed the door shut and took hold of Frank's other side. We hobbled along to the gate and I swore. There was no way he could climb over. It wasn't extremely tall, but he was losing blood and energy fast.

Then I spotted dryers and washing machines stacked up to our right. I guided us to them, and let go of Frank so I could climb up. The makeshift structure brought us right up to the tip of the fence. Blaze pushed while I hauled him up. Frank's blood seeped onto the grimy appliances, causing him to slip as we got him to the top. Blaze gave him one last shove and he was on the top with me.

"Get on the other side. I'll jump," Frank ordered through clenched teeth.

I obeyed and maneuvered to the other side easily. Frank slung one leg over, screamed, and then fell. I managed to break most of his fall, but things weren't looking good. Blaze landed right beside me and brought Frank's arm over her shoulder, leading him to the Mustang.

Once he was in the backseat, Blaze took the driver's side and I went into the back, furiously searching for anything to tie around his leg to stop the bleeding. The car rumbled to life and Blaze spun out, gravel kicking up everywhere.

"What's the damage?" Blaze yelled back to me, loud enough to overcome Frank's groans and shouts of pain.

Just as I was about to respond, Frank turned to her and said, "Not fucking well, girlie. I'm going to die."

Chapter 19

Blood covered the backseat. We were hot-boxing in the tinny scent of it. No one thought to unroll a window during all the chaos. Frank breathed deeply, drifting in and out of consciousness.

Little birdies started their singing again, probably because that Judy-Beth, whore of Satan, was dead. Trees covered in bright, summery light flashed by us as we sped to our unknown destination.

And probably our demise, I thought.

I reassured Frank many times, as I wrapped a makeshift tourniquet around his upper thigh, that he would not die and that the wound wasn't as bad as he thought.

But I knew better. His face was washed and rung. The amount of wet red everywhere confirmed a huge loss of blood. We needed to stop and assess his chances and what we would do.

Did I want to? Certainly not. Nothing was worse than acknowledging a messy, rat's nest of a problem.

"We need to get the bullets out. We need to see how big the wound is," Blaze said. "Can you tell if it's buckshot?"

Dazed, I looked at the back of her head and tried to imagine myself out of the situation. Words were coming from her general direction, but it meant nothing. My guilt was what mattered now. If I had been smarter about this whole adventure, Frank wouldn't have shotgun wounds in his leg to begin with. Old Man Meat wouldn't be resting in my large intestine.

The Mustang came to an abrupt halt, hurling my body between the two front seats. My head almost connected with the radio panel, but I managed to throw my hands up in front. All the buttons on the console dug into my hands, sending a dull pain through them despite my gloves. I heard Frank yelp in pain from the stop and Blaze gasped.

Raising my head, I looked over the dashboard down the road. There was a blockade and soldiers arming it. A Humvee, complete with mounted gun, was centered behind barbed wire and metal structures, obstructing the road. More than a few men raised rifles, pointing them at us with a mission.

They weren't the rotters we were used to. They were the righteous and holy U.S. Army.

"What is this?" I grumbled as I returned to the backseat, next to Frank.

"Maybe they've managed to hold out," Blaze offered.

"Why did you stop?"

She turned and glared at me. "What, did you think I was going to run them over? I turned a corner and there they were."

Frank moaned, sounding too much like a Z for my tastes.

Some of the soldiers jogged toward us. They appeared to be giving us the benefit of the doubt, but I wasn't returning the favor. Not after what happened with that madcap Judy-Beth.

Blaze broke my thoughts. "Let me handle this."

Before I could stop her, she was out of the car and jogging toward them, weaponless. I figured she had some kind of military-related advantage on her hands. They lowered their rifles as she neared and took turns shaking hands.

The army guys and Blaze talked for at least five minutes before she came trotting back, a pleased look on her face.

"They have the whole town under control," she explained, then looked at Frank. "They also say they have a doctor who can help."

"Good," I said. "Let's get to it."

Our new friends dragged the blockades out of the way and Blaze drove straight through, crossing a substantial bridge as we went. The same river we'd been following rushed below us, carrying strange rubble in its currents.

"This could be a trap," I said as we bumped over train tracks. A nonfunctional stoplight loomed overhead as we passed under, crossing the empty intersection. Past the intersection, to the right, was a Mexican restaurant. My stomach tensed and I swallowed down a burp of vomit.

Blaze didn't respond, but instead took a left and pulled to a stop in front of a public library. The windows were high up, beyond reaching distance, so they weren't boarded. A couple soldiers and people in civilian clothing milled about with guns. Blaze got out, slamming the door behind her before I had the chance to exit.

Irritated, I opened my door and went to the other side to get Frank. Resurrecting my caring voice, used with Gabe long ago, I told him, "It'll be okay, buddy."

Frank forced his eyes open and looked at me skeptically before shutting them.

"Come on, Bordeaux. Let's get you out of here."

I maneuvered him out of the backseat. His bad leg collapsed under him, forcing me to wrap both arms around him for support. Blaze jogged back to us and put one of Frank's arms over her shoulders, alleviating me. I got into a better position with his other arm around me, and we were on our way, dragging him to where Blaze directed.

"Their resident doctor is in the library. They told me he'll do whatever he can to help Frank. No cost."

"Well, thank the heavens for that. I don't have my wallet on me," I said, anxiety growing as Frank's weight grew heavier. He had no ability to support himself. I looked down and saw a trail of blood behind us. How could Frank still be alive? He was losing a gallon a minute.

There was a woman behind the checkout counter, looking all the part of a librarian. The library, overall, appeared to be in great condition. Even the aged, distinct scent of books was intact. When we approached, she rose and ushered us into a closed off study room.

The room had been converted into a doctor's office, complete with a raised gurney. Mobile shelves lined the walls, filled with shiny, promising medical supplies. A man waited for us, a walkie-talkie hanging from a cord on his neck, just below his huge auburn beard.

"My name is Dr. Kalman." He waved toward the gurney. "Place him down and leave. I'll take a look."

"I'm not leaving. I'm not!"

Blaze grabbed me by the arm and shook her head. "Let him do what he can, Sinclair. You'll only get in the way."

I opened my mouth then closed it. She was right. There was no room for me to be in there. No matter how badly I wanted to, I couldn't help, so I let Blaze guide me from the room.

Once outside, Kalman dropped a sheet over the window, pointedly preventing me from watching what was going to transpire. Grinding my teeth, I was a half second away from going berserk when Blaze grabbed my wounded shoulder and squeezed.

My hiss of pain was cut off when she said, "Get it the fuck together. Being a little bitch isn't going to help anything."

"You kids look hungry," the plump librarian said, appearing soon after. "Follow me."

Hungry? I had human meat in my belly, Frank was dying, and I wasn't sure of anything beyond that. My stomach bubbled and I fought back the urge to vomit again.

Blaze let go of my shoulder as though she hadn't caused me excruciating pain. She smiled at the lady.

"We'd appreciate it. Thank you."

We trailed behind her through the musty library, going through the rows of books. On the way to wherever we were going, the woman told us how Sultan managed to survive.

"A military convoy was passing through early on, and just decided to stay. They destroyed the bridge leading into Sultan, the Highway 2 one, so no traffic could get through. The monsters tried going through the river, but it was spring and flood season. They all got swept away."

The lady, who introduced herself as Pamela, continued, "No one was going west into the big cities, so there was no traffic coming from the east. We were going to blow that other bridge—the one you came over on—today. You're lucky you made it in time. One of the boys couldn't find the C4 detonator."

She laughed a big, jolly laugh then sighed. "We have strict rules here. It helps keeps everyone in place, so no rioting or anything like that happens. The curfew is at dusk, and that's when everyone goes back to the safe houses for the night."

"Safe houses? How many survivors are there?" I asked.

"Oh, there are exactly 159 of us. The safe houses are the ones we put the most effort into fortifying. The library is one of them, and then the elementary school down the street. It houses most of us. There are a few outposts, too, near the entrances to Sultan."

As we spoke, I worked off my Hellstorm gloves and stretched my fingers. Having the digits exposed to the air felt strange, but I savored it. I hadn't taken them off once since last night, when we crashed at the house in Monroe.

She took us up a flight of stairs and into another study room. Inside were piles and shelves of non-perishable food items. A small box of brightly colored packages caught my eye, and my spirits lifted.

"I see you have some candy." I casually made my way over to the goods. "Mind if I…"

Pam eyed me in disbelief then nodded. "I suppose you can take some. No one eats it. It's so unhealthy."

I shrugged. "I have a sweet tooth."

There were some of my favorites: Sour Patch Kids, Dots, Pixie Stix, and Red Vines. I shoved the delights in my vest and pants pockets. My hand hit the can of sweetened condensed milk as I rammed these into a pocket, reminding me of earlier, but I shoved the memory away.

Blaze took a bottle of water and a few protein bars. Even though I didn't want to, I did the same. I'd wash away the gross flavor of bar later with sugar.

"You know," Pam said, "you three are welcome to stay here with us. A lot of people passing through decide to stay. We welcome anyone."

Expecting this, I put a saccharine smile on and declined. "That's very kind of you, but we already have somewhere we're headed. I've got my heart set on it."

Blaze put on her people-voice. "It's true. We just want to head into the mountains. You understand, right?"

The woman's chins quadrupled then returned to double as she nodded. She even went so far as to pat us both on the shoulder as we gnawed on our stale lunch.

"You can stay as long as you want. Why don't you meet some of the folks around here? They'll be glad to see someone new."

Grin still plastered on my face, I said, "I'd be delighted."

* * *

Four hours later, we'd received a full tour of the town, walking while meeting all the significant tenants.

Most of the buildings were condemned by the Sultan leaders. Entry was expressly forbidden. Pam explained that some of the houses were vandalized, boarded from the inside, or contained gruesome scenes no one was willing to clean up or fix. Xs were spray painted on the doors of these places, while blue circles signified a safe location.

The streets were clean and pleasant, completely void of the gore and destruction back in Monroe and Seattle. Sultan looked more the part of a ghost town than one in the midst of the living dead. Pamela explained that people felt safer when things looked normal.

Normal is over, I thought. People need to realize that. But to dear Pam, I said nothing.

We met the unofficial but proud leader of the survivors. His name was Jack DeFrank, who fit the stereotype of impromptu-apocalyptic-leader to the letter. Even his handshake was what I expected—firm, but not violent. What with his five o'clock shadow, square jaw, and a propensity for wanting to save everyone, he seemed to have stepped straight from the silver screen.

During our bland tour, Frank was on my mind, but Pam kept telling me to be patient. She told us they'd radio her when the doctor had news. Every time the walkie-talkie around her neck crackled to life, I assumed the worse, but hoped for the best.

Pam took us to a quaint, white house far from the library. It was set far back from an unkempt lawn, already crispy brown from the summer heat. Each window was neatly boarded, but the front door was blue-circled and unlocked. Behind it was a thick forest and the sound of a river nearby. Pam went in as though she owned the place. It turned out she did.

"This is my house. I don't stay here anymore."

Blaze asked, "Why not?"

Pam blushed and waved her hand in the air. "I'm afraid of the forest. It's very small, just a patch, and then the river is there. But I don't like it. I brought you here so you could take a shower. Maybe take a nap."

"A shower?" I said eagerly. "How?"

"Oh, well, I'm not on city water. It isn't hot because I don't have power or anything, but it's still a shower. Usually everyone comes here for a shower once every few days."

"Thank you, Pamela. You're so kind," Blaze flattered.

Responding well to the compliment, she gave us a toothy grin before walking to the door. "It's nothing, really. I'll come get you as soon as I find something out about your friend."

When she left, I took a look about the place. It was one story and looked like it belonged to Pamela. White lace on everything. The little sitting room had a love seat and two recliners situated around a glass coffee table adorned with fake, bright daffodils. Huge skylights illuminated the room, as well as the joined dining room and kitchen. Despite the situation we were all in, the house was extremely clean.

"She is nice," I murmured.

Blaze already set off down the short hallway with two doors. Both were open to reveal a bathroom and a bedroom. "I'm taking a shower. Try to relax. Everything will be fine."

Not bothering with a reply, I slouched onto the sofa and unlaced my boots. Feeling too burdened, I continued stripping, and took off my holsters and vest, too. It felt good and I relished in it. From the bathroom a gurgling sound started up, then the continuous drone of a shower.

Just to keep my mind on something mundane so I could relax, I counted the seconds Blaze was in the shower.

One hundred sixty…

I realized she was definitely naked in the shower.

Two hundred twenty…

She probably had a fantastic body. It was hard to tell through her tactical gear, but I'd bet money that body was as lean and mean as she was.

Three hundred forty…

Did she think I was thinking about her? Didn't women know about that kind of thing? What if she wanted me to come in there?

Three-hundred-something…

I chuckled. I'd completely lost it. Here I was, in a stranger's house, while my father-figure was dying, contemplating whether Blaze Wright wanted me to come ravish her.

Just the thought of Frank sobered me. I needed to clear my mind, because thinking about him wasn't going to change anything or speed up time.

After forcibly removing myself from the comfortable couch, I walked around the house. After only a few minutes I found myself in the bedroom, looking at a collection of photos on a long, oak dresser. All of the photos had Pamela, some with other people, but most of them at recognizable locations: a pyramid, the Eiffel Tower, Big Ben. She looked young and thin in the majority, but the same plump woman I knew graced a few of them. Pam was a world traveler, then.

The bed wore a pristine white comforter, and two white-lace covered end tables sat on either side. Useless lamps rested on both. One had a worn paperback on it. I walked over and picked it up. It was a silly romance novel about a duchess falling in love with a thief. Forbidden love.

Noises from the bathroom ceased, and I turned to see the door swing open. Blaze came out in a loose white undershirt and a pair of small men's boxers. Shocked by her lack of clothing, I turned back around and stared intently at the satin lampshade in front of me.

Her bare feet scuffed over the carpet as she went over to the bed, then came the rustling of covers pulled back. From the corner of my eye, I saw her pale body slide beneath.

"I'm going to sleep." She plumped up a pillow before laying her wet head on it.

"I'll take a shower then."

I walked out of the bedroom and into the bath. A high up, rectangular window produced a muted natural light. The bathroom had a white, feminine theme.

Gripping the edge of the counter, I stared into the big mirror. Someone looked like they'd been in traffic for twenty hours straight, had an absurdly long flight layover, or taken a trip to hell and back. That someone was me. My face was scabbed and puffy from hitting the wall at the prison.

Weeks of golden stubble graced my jaw. I'd never been great at growing a beard for some reason, so I didn't look like a mountain man. My eyes were saggy and dull—the usual hard, crisp green muted and reluctant. Even my naturally reddish hair looked flat. I inhaled deeply then exhaled. My lungs protested from the action, but it hurt nicely so I did it again.

Careful so as not to enrage my myriad of angry wounds, I stripped off my dirty clothes and tossed them onto the pink tiled floor. The cool air of the bathroom refreshed my skin, and I relished in the normalcy of what I was about to do.

Since I was seventeen I'd been taking cold showers, so when the icy water struck my back I didn't even wince. The water felt blissful, and I didn't mind sorting through a profound collection of girly shower products.

Scalp Nourishing Conditioner? Sure, I'd try it.

Body Slimming Scrub? Well, I certainly needed some scrubbing.

Skin Enriching Body Wash? I'd love to be enriched.

By the time I applied everything I could, I felt like a million bucks. There was even a Costco package of toothbrushes under the sink that I helped myself to. I wrapped a towel around my waist and sat on the bathroom counter.

Everything about making it to Frank's cabin hadn't been what I had expected. When he first convinced me of his plan, I thought it would be a breeze. Who knew I'd meet other survivors? I thought I was the only survivor. That showed how closed-minded and self righteous I was.

To me, there was an unreasonable amount of obstacles between me and my destination. People, emotions, situations—they all stopped me. I hadn't planned on any of it.

Speaking of plans, I hadn't planned on meeting someone like Blaze or meeting up with Frank again. But it happened, and a part of me was grateful for it.

A battery-operated clock directly across from me claimed it was 7:00 p.m. In a few hours, it would be dark, and I wanted to leave before then. Woefully, I redressed and exited the bathroom.

Blaze was out cold.

As I stood in the doorway, I noted when she was asleep, and didn't have a cigarette in her mouth, she wasn't too bad to look at. The subtle scowl was replaced with a calm slackness I rarely saw. She looked younger then, and I wondered how old she really was.

I wished the Mustang were here. The radios were in it, and I wanted to leave one for her so she knew where I was going. Not like she would have to guess very hard.

Booted up, I left the house and began my walk back to the library. I passed Joseph, a man I'd met earlier, and told him about Blaze in the house. He said he'd patrol it, since I had no way to lock it up. Maybe a community of survivors wasn't such a bad thing, as long as they weren't out of their minds.

Nah, I thought. They'll go crazy eventually.

The sun was turning golden to the west, while dark, foreboding clouds rolled in from the north. Summer had glorious thunder and lightning storms. The air was always electric and smelled wet. Soon the hot asphalt would be wet, releasing its quintessential summery scent. As a rule, when I was a teenager, I'd stop and relish in such things.

Not this time. There was something more important on my mind: Frank.

* * *

"I'm sorry, Mr. Sinclair. I've done all I can," Dr. Kalman said. "He isn't going to make it."

Bile rose in my throat. I squeezed my eyes shut and tried to die right then.

When I arrived at the library, Pamela welcomed me with a sad smile and a pat on the back. She even offered me a small speech about the afterlife, but I couldn't pay attention to a word of it.

I walked into the makeshift hospital room and knew, right then, that Frank really was going to die.

He isn't going to make it. Dr. Kalman's words ran through my head as I stared at Frank. Each limb was tied twice to the gurney, and a rope encircled his waist.

Did this kind of thing happen often in Sultan? I couldn't help but wonder since they seemed so prepped for it. Someone wasn't going to make it, and a loved one wanted to see them one last time before they turned into...

Frank opened his eyes and found me sitting on a folding chair next to him. His pant leg was torn up to the hip, bloody leg bandaged, but it didn't matter.

"What are you doing here, boy? I figured you'd be with your lady friend." He grinned weakly, then lifted his chin to look at his restraints. "I understand."

"Understand?"

"The map to my cabin is in my knapsack in the car. I wrote some extra directions down, just in case."

"What do you understand?"

He spoke right over me. "You'll know it right when you see it. There's color-coded deadbolts on the door. The keys are in my knapsack, too. Color coded."

I bolted out of my chair. "What do you understand?"

Lips pursed, he shut his eyes and heaved a long sigh. "I'm gonna die, Cyrus. I understand that. Doc said some of the buckshot hit the femoral artery, or some doctor bullshit. I don't know, but it don't matter. It's time I checked out."

Tried as I might to deny it, it was true. My only friend—the only man I respected—was about to die in a library because of a crazy lady on a back road to Sultan.

"You'll take care of me when I go, right? I wouldn't want a stranger doing me in. I'd appreciate it, boy."

I nodded.

* * *

Francis fell in and out of consciousness for the next few hours. I waited by his bedside, listening to every jumbled word that came out of his mouth. At one point it grew dark, and Pamela brought in a Coleman lantern. It cast an unfriendly white-blue glow on everything, creating deep, cavernous shadows around us.

Then he stopped talking. Moving. Breathing. Minutes passed before violent thrashing and gnashing teeth ensued. Francis Jackson Bordeaux was undead. His eyes were cloudy and white, his skin grayed. All he wanted now was to eat me.

Pain shot up my arm as I released my 9mm from its holster and pointed it, hand shaking, at Frank's head.

I pulled the trigger. "I'm sorry." And I left.

Chapter 20

People I'd known for less than a day tried to stop me and give their consolations. Deep down it enraged me, and I wanted to take a shotgun to each of their heads, screaming, and then beat their bodies into a pulp.

But all they saw was a stony face unwilling to give them the time of day. As it should be. Indulging my fantasies meant wasting ammunition, let's be honest. Sometimes it's a matter of practicality that you didn't go busting caps everywhere.

I threw open the Mustang door and roared off back to Pam's house, ready to pick up Blaze and get the hell out of there. If I never saw Sultan again, it would be far too soon.

Somewhere in the backseat I heard scratching, and I knew it was Pickle disputing the jerky motions of the car.

Blaze was waiting outside on the curb, sitting with her elbows resting on her knees. The guy I talked to, Joseph, sat next to her. He had a walkie-talkie dangling from his neck, so I assumed they both knew the news. Even if they didn't, I was in no fucking mood to talk about it.

Feeling bitter and livid, I slammed on the brakes and skidded in the middle of the road, stopping right in front of the pair.

"Get the fuck in. We're leaving."

Joseph dropped his head and stared at the cement. A portable lantern to his right illuminated the small space he and Blaze occupied and showed the uncomfortable expression on his face

Almost as though she had an off switch, her face went blank as Wright stood and stalked to the passenger side and got in swiftly. Not a word escaped her lips as we sped off. The headlights revealed survivors gathering on the roadside, waving and shouting for us to stop. Their pleas fell on deaf ears as I turned onto Highway 2, a grand stretch of clear asphalt in front of me.

As we cleared the outskirts of Sultan, the thunderstorm I predicted came to fruition. It was loud and irate, dropping water on us like bricks, clapping its thunder until my ears rang. Lighting flashed and exposed snapshots of the forest flanking the road.

Only minutes flew by, but it seemed like forever. My jaw hurt from clenching my teeth. My head felt big and sore, like I had a record breaking head cold. I had to make a conscious decision to keep breathing. The scent of ozone filled my nostrils each time I inhaled and I took it all in, focusing on it rather than on other problems.

Rain fell too hard for the windshield wipers to keep up. Visibility was poor. My face was almost pressed against the windshield as I tried to make out the road. Not like it mattered, since there wasn't a single car in sight. What did matter, now, though? Frank was dead. I might not be able to find our way to the cabin, despite his repeated directions and the map. It should've been apparent to everyone on the fucking planet that I was as inept as a quadriplegic trying to ice skate. No offense.

Just to add to my misery, the Mustang began to slow. I looked at the gas gauge and saw the car was running on fumes. Actually, it wasn't running anymore.

We glided to a stop.

Then I snapped. I didn't realize I was screaming and beating the steering wheel until Blaze grabbed my hands and forced me to stop. Wrath consuming me, I pushed her away and shoved the door open, walking into the cold night. The Mustang's headlights cut through the darkness and illuminated some of the barren road.

"It's my fucking fault!" I roared at the sky, then kicked the wheel of the car.

A car door opened and slammed, but I didn't pay attention. Rain pelted my entire body, drenching my hair and clothing. A brief thunderclap stopped my rant, but then I was back at it once again.

"I should've known. I should've known whatever was in that house was fucked up! I could've put it together, but I didn't. Now Frank is dead. I shot him!"

Through the white noise of rainfall, boots splashed. Blaze stood across from me. The two headlights separated us and lit her face. Raven hair clung to her cheeks and water sluiced down her nose. I watched as a drop caught the light and fell.

"This isn't how it was supposed to go." I paced back and forth. "We were supposed to just make it. We're too good to just get shot like that! We know how to get guns, how to analyze situations. What the fuck is this? Why—why is this—I just—"

Despite it being a good dinner bell for the undead, I screamed until my throat went raw. Once my rage petered out, I went to the hood of the Mustang and slammed both fists against the metal as hard as I could. Pain went through my forearms and up into my shoulders.

"I can't handle this pressure. Somehow, Gabe became my responsibility. I thought Frank was unstoppable, but he's an old man. I was responsible for him, too, but I was blind. I'm fucking ignorant when it comes to being a leader!" I was too far gone, because then I added, "And I'm responsible for you now, too. And I'm going to fuck up with you, just like I did with them."

A gentle hand pressed against my shoulder. Embarrassment edged its way into my rage. Naturally I had to have the first hissy fit in my life in front of an ex-Marine named Beatrice Wright, in the rain, during the undead apocalypse. Normally even if I was in turmoil on the inside, I wouldn't show it. I was flawless at everything I did: killing, surviving, and keeping things inside. Normally, I was fundamentally perfect. In my opinion.

My name is Cyrus V. Sinclair. The V stands for vainglory.

Even though it pained me to do so, I turned and looked at Blaze. Her face softened, lacking the steel aura that typically chilled it.

"It wasn't your fault," she said, even as I tried to cut her off. "There was no way to stop her from shooting him. There was no way you could've known she was a lunatic. Bordeaux understood that."

When she finished, I tried to choke back an unfamiliar sensation, but it came in waves. I was sobbing. Aggressively, Blaze grabbed me by the shoulder and spun me into an unyielding embrace.

"He knew you aren't the sociopath you paint yourself to be. If you were, you wouldn't be crying right now." She squeezed me tighter when I tried to refute the tears. "You can be a cocksucker any day of the week, but someone who meant a lot to you just died. It isn't unreasonable to be upset."

I dropped my head into the crook of her neck and laughed, but it came out as a wail. Hesitantly, I brought my arms up around her waist and returned the hug. She had a point, and I was beginning to think it was a good idea to let my façade down every once in a while.

Blaze's clothes smelled like cigarettes, but her skin held the scents of Pam's floral bath products. Underneath it all was a smell I was unused to but knew. It was the scent of a woman. The perfume comforted me, and I unabashedly inhaled it, pressing my face into the damp skin of her neck.

"He was my idol. He accepted me when no one else did" I whispered. "Now he's gone."

"Depends on what you believe in," she countered as she rubbed circles on my back. I barely felt it through my shirt and vest. "But let me tell you something. If he's watching you from some redneck place up in the clouds, what would he say?"

After a moment, I replied, "He'd say, 'Boy, you'd better get your ass moving 'cause we ain't got time to waste.'"

Her body shook as she laughed. "I think he'd say that too."

Very aware of our proximity, I dropped my arms and took a baby step back from her. Her dark eyes caught mine and she reached out, pushing hair back from my forehead. Blaze's hands felt hot and damp against my skin.

"There should be a gas station up here. Frank mentioned it," I said, breaking the silence.

"Well, let's hop the fuck to it, Sinclair."

* * *

A short distance from where we were lie a small pocket of buildings. On the left was a McDonalds and a Subway. Both looked out of place and almost funny. They were so normal and untouched. It was as though they were just closed for the night.

On the right was a lonely Chevron, dark and threatening, and a huge auto body shop. The latter was one huge rectangle in shape, with a single door and window in the front.

Blaze and I stopped pushing the Mustang and I cranked the emergency brake. My arms were stiff from pushing it for so long. She didn't complain or show any discomfort. After closing the car door, I paused. I didn't know how to siphon gas like Frank did. Maybe out of another car, but not an electric pump.

A strange make of car I'd never seen before sat by one of the gas pumps. It was metallic orange and vaguely resembled a baby minivan. We walked up behind it, two pumps down, and waited for signs of the Zs. None came. No moaning, no groaning, and no shuffling. Good thing that baby minivan was here.

"We need to find some kind of tubing so I can get gas out of that car," I told Blaze.

She gazed at the ominous convenience store. "That place looks unscathed. Maybe we can find something in there?"

I looked at it, too, and shrugged. "We could give it a try."

Blaze grabbed her carbine from the back, but I opted for my 9mm. It would be too hard to handle the flashlight and a larger gun. I checked the clip and made sure I had extras in my vest before moving forward.

The glass doors of the convenience store still had an "Open" sign hanging on it. I went first, pushing the door inward. Without a sound, it smoothly gave way.

I gave Blaze a look and said, "This is too easy. Stay alert."

Not an item was misplaced or a shelf broken. My flashlight landed upon pristine aisles and a clean, black and white checkered floor. Only the smell—rotted hotdogs and pizza—was out of place.

It was eerie in there. I remembered the incident in Monroe, when a zombie almost got me. That place had seemed safe enough. I knew I had to be more careful now.

Motioning for Blaze to search the right half of the store, I set off for the left, searching for the automotive section most gas stations had.

After only a few moments, I found myself in the candy aisle. Hundreds of colorfully packaged delights stared back at me, and if there was one thing I really needed that night… Well, it was a quick sweet treat.

My pockets already held candy from Sultan, but why eat that when I had some right in front of me? I had to conserve my resources, after all. I ran my hand down the crinkly, smooth selection of candy and stopped at a box of Sour Patch Kids.

Now I only needed some orange Hi-C.

Tube for siphoning forgotten, I began searching for the drink section, which wasn't too far away. Little orange Hi-C juice boxes beckoned me. I set my handgun on top of the shelves, tore the crinkly packages open and got to work, alternating handfuls of sour candies with gulps of sweet juice.

Halfway through the snack, shuffling and a scream came from somewhere in the back of the station. I dropped everything, grabbed my gun and flashlight, and ran in the direction of the yelling. It only took a moment to find the back door and kick it open.

A greasy, teenage kid had Blaze by the hair. He was swinging from a ceiling fan in a back stock room, not unlike the one in Monroe I'd been attacked in previously. My flashlight revealed mottled blue skin that was peeled and sagged. Diseased mouth open and ruined hands clenching eagerly, he didn't realize he'd hung himself and couldn't get anywhere.

(Not like I thought about it every day, but if I were going to kill myself, I'd make sure I could fulfill my zombie duties afterwards.)

"If I had a camera, this would be a Hallmark moment." I laughed, not making a move to help her. She could help herself.

Blaze reached up and grabbed the Zs wrists. Skin rubbed off, revealing rotted muscle underneath. Her hands slipped and came away with dark, clotted blood.

I noticed her gun right in front of her, just a few feet away. She must've dropped it when the kid got her.

"Okay." I sighed in defeat as I raised my gun.

One shot later, the undead was truly dead. My bullet entered his skull through his right eye and went straight through into the wall behind him. Blood and sticky, dark gore coated the wall and dripped down from the back of his head.

Drip. Drip.

Blaze rubbed her head vigorously and bent over to pick up her rifle. With a displeased glare, she stalked out of the back room and into the store.

"There's nothing here we can use for the car," she called, drawing me out of the room, too.

She stood in front of my predicted auto section. There was nothing there we could use either—just windshield wiper fluid, motor oil, and air fresheners. I frowned, rubbing my hand along my jaw.

"We could try that auto shop," I offered. "They must have something. They might even have gas cans."

Blaze agreed, but stopped me as I turned to leave.

"There's a ton of food here. We should take anything we can."

Why didn't I think of that? We had zero food, and there was no telling how long it would take to get to the cabin. At this rate it might take days.

I jogged over to the cashier counter and found a neat stack of moderately sized plastic bags. Behind the counter were endless brands of cigarettes, and I knew someone who'd want to take them—but for my own benefit, I kept my mouth shut.

Blaze and I roamed the aisles, shoving anything of use into the bags. She wandered off to the register, and I watched as she withdrew a knife and started prying at a display case lock.

"What are you doing?"

She looked back. "I'm out of cigarettes. Why stop later when I can get them here?"

"You're kidding," I griped. "I'm not sure why you're still smoking. Don't you see it's contradictory to our entire goal right now?"

Chuckling, Blaze shook her head. "I don't know what you mean."

"For starters it's bad for you. You're going to get lung cancer, which could kill you. Right now we're trying to survive. You're being counterproductive."

Just to spite me, she stopped and lit up. Smoke snaking from her mouth, she said, "You're looking kind of fat, Cyrus. That candy vice of yours is really taking its toll, isn't it?"

I glared. "I'm not getting cancer from sugar."

"You win some and you lose some, I guess." She shrugged. "I smoke. I want more cigarettes, plain and fucking simple."

Some people justified addictions, but she wasn't one of them. She smoked like a chimney. That was that. I stopped gaping at her and turned away. Her bad habit made me stressed out.

Eating candy was my mechanism against stress. I ripped open another package of Sour Patch Kids and ate them by the mouthful as I finished filling bags. Blaze finished stocking a bag with multiple brands of smokes. I guess she didn't discriminate. Good for her.

By the end of our raid, we used up all of the plastic sacks. With less caution than usual, we made trips back and forth to fill the empty trunk of the Mustang. Things were looking up.

We decided not to take another chance with our vehicle and pushed it behind the auto body shop, entirely out of sight from the highway. It was convenient since the back of the building had one large garage opening and a back door, which was hanging open. The Mustang would be hidden and we'd still have fast access to it. I went first again and moved to the door, which was a pit of darkness. If any noise came from inside, I wouldn't have been able to tell. The roof was made of metal, and the pounding rain was amplified inside.

Flashlight raised, I shone it into the abyss.

It was a small office space with a single, shut door near a reception desk directly across from me. There was no sign of a living or undead anywhere. I took a few steps inside and waited for an attack, which never came. A leather couch was against the left wall with a coffee table in front, the last editions of car magazines stacked on it.

With the sound of Blaze's squelching boots behind me, I ventured in farther. She shut the door, the sound of it barely audible through the noise of rain against the thin roof.

So far so good, I thought, as I walked over to the only door. It was unlocked, and lead into an open garage space.

Everything in the shop was typical: cars on hydraulic lifts, parts on every surface and shelf, and, sure enough, familiar red gas cans. Things were working out, for we also found a hose.

Blaze and I searched the rest of the area and happened upon nothing else of interest, but since we found what we wanted no one was disappointed. Anything beyond that would have been superfluous.

There were only two cans, but each carried 5 gallons, which would be more than enough for the trip to the cabin. One of the cars in the garage had almost a full tank of gas, saving us the trip back out to the orange car. We carried the filled containers into the reception office and I paused to yawn.

"You tired?" Blaze asked as she set down her can.

I shrugged. "I'll live."

She went to the front door and slid the deadbolt into place before going to the single, rectangular window in the room and closing the blinds. After she secured the immediate area, she turned back to me. The light of her flashlight was pointed down, but it reflected off the white tile and created an ambient light.

"It's been a long day," she said. "Now's a convenient time to sleep, so I think we should."

"We're so close. We're almost there." I tried to keep my voice firm. My drowsiness agreeing with the notion of a long nap.

Blaze shook her head and went to the couch, plopping down and turning off her flashlight.

"Don't be unreasonable. I'll even let you be chivalrous and sleep on the floor."

Shining my flashlight near her, I spotted a grin on her lips.

I sat on the floor next to her. "That's supposed to be a privilege, huh?"

"Sure is." She reached down and took my light, clicking it off. "Go to sleep. We'll head out first thing in the morning."

The right thing to do would've been to continue disagreeing, but I felt strangely comfortable as I leaned against the couch. Maybe a little nap would be fine? I was drowsy. I'd just close my eyes for a second.

* * *

Guilt still plagued me and kept me from shutting my eyes, let alone sleeping. I turned on my side once again, my clothes brushing over the tile floor.

When I fell asleep earlier, it was only for an hour, until my body, without consulting my mind, decided that was a very sensible amount of sleep. Since then, I'd tossed on the hard tile, trying to find a comfortable position. No fortune on that front.

"What's the issue?"

I sat up and looked in the direction of Blaze's voice. There was no light to make out definite shapes, but I could sense her position.

"Can't sleep," I muttered and crawled onto the couch.

In the darkness I bumped into her. She was laying down, but I heard her move until she was upright. I sat next to her.

"How about I talk you to sleep? You'll be under in no time."

"I suppose."

"Get comfortable," she said, feeling for me and guiding me into a reclined position. My legs dangled off the edge of the couch while my head rested in her lap. I don't know where she got it from, but a moment later a pill pressed against my lips. I opened and dry-swallowed it, not bothering to question what it was.

"What do you feel like hearing?"

I couldn't answer. I was too busy thinking about the comfort of the sofa and the warmth of Blaze's body. Hesitant fingers found my hair and stroked it. We were caught up in intimacy once again, and I wasn't going to stop it.

"How about the story of your life?" I wasn't entirely serious, but she decided to do just that and start from the beginning.

"My dad was a marine. When my mom was twenty she got pregnant, and my dad figured he could only have sons. He was just that much of a man. He wanted a boy who could carry on the family name, be a marine, and do him proud. But, as you can see, he didn't get a boy. It's funny, too, because he had an illegitimate daughter, my half-sister, during their marriage. He should've known he might get another one."

I knew where this was going. I made an m-hmm noise, and she continued.

"My father still treated me like a boy and pretended I was one. I did baseball instead of ballet. I had toy guns instead of dollies." There was a whisper of venom in her voice.

"When I was eight, my mom had a boy—his name was Beau—and my father was beyond pleased. About thirteen years later, it was evident Beau had no interest in being the man my father planned he'd be. I was twenty-one and had no prospects except for the military. So I signed up.

"I can't tell you how many letters I received from my father and mother. Mom didn't care that Beau was gay, but dad sure did. 'Fucking faggot' he'd call him. 'A disgrace to the family.' All my father had was me, a girl who lived like a man. No matter how much of a man I was, it didn't matter."

"You mean he didn't even acknowledge what you did for him? That you were serving because of him?"

Blaze went silent then said, "He did in the end. Just a few months before all this zombie-shit started happening, I went to see him in the nursing home. I'd been in the marines for about seven years, not like he knew. I told him I just got back from Iraq and was finished. I wasn't serving anymore. I told him I'd done it all for him because I wanted to make him proud.

"He said to me, 'Bea, you've made me proud since the day you were born.'"

"Did you believe him?"

I felt her body move, so I figured she shrugged. "I guess I do. It would give me closure if I did, wouldn't it?"

"It would, but only if you really believe it. Otherwise you'd be tricking yourself." Then I changed the subject. "Where's your brother? Do you know?"

"No. Probably dead, like everyone else."

I caught onto her hesitance. "What? Do you think he's alive?"

"When we were young, we used to visit an island in the Puget Sound off the coast of Samish Island. Beau and I joked about how it would be the first place we went if something bad happened because it's so isolated," she said.

"You think he's there?"

"I don't know."

After that, she built a wall and sealed off any more conversation of her family. Instead, she told me about being in the military and her brief stint in college.

I was interested in her story, but my eyelids were heavy and her hands on me was soothing. Just as she finished a story about a chicken and a mess hall, I fell fast asleep.

Chapter 21

Two things woke me up: the absence of rain and a banging noise. Disoriented from the sleeping pill Blaze gave me, I opened my eyes and tried to remember where I was.

The noise was coming from my right. I propped myself up on the bed and looked at the closed window. Minimal morning light filtered through the closed blinds. A lone shadowy figure stood behind the window. It was the source of the noise.

As I continued to watch, a hand touched the glass and slid down. It was the impact of flesh against the window that woke me.

Just one of them, I thought. *Not a big deal.*

Blaze was still asleep, so I took the moment to steal a long look at her. She was in the corner of the couch, legs tucked under her. There was just enough light to make out the gentle slope of her nose and the scar down her cheek. She was beautiful in an unconventional way. Or maybe just to me?

Crazy thoughts. Closing my eyes, I took a deep breath and removed myself from the couch. Blaze coughed and rustled, signs of her awakening.

"There's a Z out there."

She sniffed and wiped a sleeve against her nose. "Just one?"

I shrugged.

"There's rarely just one, Sinclair."

"Well, go take a look."

Blaze strolled over to the window and inched open a blind. Her face dropped into a frown. She sniffed again.

"If I told you I was right, would you be crushed?"

"Crushed is an understatement." I groaned, bringing my hands up to cover my face. "How many are there?"

"More than we can handle. They're surrounding the car."

Giving in, I looked out, and stopped counting after twenty. Some of the Zs had McDonald's uniforms on, which explained why they were here. They must've seen us last night and made their way over. Anyone who lacked life would've seen them migrating and joined the club. But this many?

I noticed figures coming from the forest. What lie in or far from it was beyond me. But there were undead straggling from its shady depths, onto the concrete driveway our getaway car was on.

"We still need to put gas in the car," I said. "As you can see, there are major preventatives going on."

"Just one," Blaze said as she rifled around. She pulled out a cigarette and brought it to her lips. "They're out there. That's the only problem. If they leave, we don't have an issue."

One flick of a lighter and an inhale later, smoke billowed from her nostrils. She grinned.

"Ah, cigarettes. The breakfast of champions," I jabbed. "I take it you have a plan?"

"Affirmative. By the looks of it, they're all slows. I'll run out and lead them away. When the coast is clear, you exit and take out any stragglers. Fill the tank up. Turn the car on, fire two shots, and I'll be on my way."

Blaze taking the lead on this didn't sit well with me, but she wanted to and I wouldn't stop her. Instead, I nodded and took out my handgun. I cursed myself for not bringing in a better weapon.

I guess, though, only one bullet was needed to kill a zombie. One shot, one kill. Caliber and speed didn't matter.

"Good luck," I said as she unlocked the door.

"I don't need luck," she said as she flung the door open and ran into the midst of some shocked undead.

Even though I wanted to watch, I slammed the door shut and locked it, back pressed against the solid metal of it.

Outside the familiar, eager moans started up. Blaze's running faded away, and after a few minutes, all the other noises also.

I checked the window and, sure enough, the slows had cleared into the forest. If I didn't take the opportunity to fill the car now, I might not get another. The idea of being holed up in the garage didn't appeal to me one bit.

Taking the inexorable chance, I dashed from the office and into the drizzly morning. Crisp air filled my lungs as I closed the short distance between myself and the Mustang. Once I arrived, I set to work filling the tank. Gasoline glugged, and the noise was far too loud for my tastes.

The staccato sound of bullets echoed from the forest. Birds took to the air, fluttering in panic as they escaped.

There was no reason to worry. Blaze could handle herself, and a few rounds didn't mean anything. She probably killed some of them. No need to worry.

Moments later the tank was filled. Pickle came out of nowhere and sat primly on the passenger's seat. Her white fur looked matted and dirty, but other than that her psychological well being seemed just fine. She stared at me through the window, but I turned away as I started the car and fired two rounds.

Time went by. Another round was fired somewhere in the forest. It could've been my ears playing tricks, but I could've sworn I heard a yell as well. If I waited, it could result in Blaze's death. I deviated from our plan.

"Why me?" I grabbed a more formidable weapon from the backseat.

Generic shotgun in hand, I left the Mustang and started for the forest. A few slows hung around the edges of the trees.

Predictably, their heads turned when they caught sound and sight of me. They're bodies lurched forward and their hands rose.

I ran straight into the trees, branches slapping my face until I broke into a small clearing. Noises were everywhere: twigs breaking and moving, zombies groaning. But none of the noises indicated where Blaze had gone.

Running around aimlessly in the forest seemed like a terrible idea, and that's because it was. My body was tense and the situation was dour. Blaze could be at the Mustang now, while I traveled deeper into the woods to find her. One bad call would unravel all the progress we'd made.

"Can't get me up here, you fucking cocksuckers!"

Ah. A mouth like that belonged to one woman in particular—Blaze Wright.

I followed her voice (which continued to insult the Zs) and found her not too far away. Using a thick bramble of bushes and a dead log as cover, I peered over its edge to assess the situation.

A score of zombies were gathered around a tree, looking up hungrily at my homicidal partner in crime. Blaze was lax, smoking a cigarette and peering up into the sky. She wedged herself between the thick branches of an oak, assault rifle slung carelessly over one shoulder.

Even if she heard my two shots, she couldn't have escape from the tree. The look on her face showed resignation. Didn't she know I'd come looking for her? Or did she have a plan?

"One, two, three, four! Who do you love?" she shouted down to the Zs, then cupped her hand to her ear dramatically. "The Marine Corps. That's right."

It was all very amusing, but I had to get the undead away and her down. A few months ago I would've left her, but when you fall in love, things change.

Love?

My mouth dropped open. Where did that come from? Love? The lack of sleep, food, and sanity must've been getting to me because love wasn't in my vocabulary when it came to a woman. Especially one I'd only known for a few days.

I erased every thought from my mind and dove out of the bushes, gun up, and a scream in my throat. That was one way to get things off your mind—risk your life boldly. Excuse me, unwisely.

Zombies turned, eyeing their newer and easier target. The closest one to me was a fat woman with thoroughly charred skin. Glistening shards of glass protruded from the right side of her face and neck. Most of her scalp was gone, revealing skull. A burned and ragged sundress completed her ghastly appearance.

I pulled the trigger and blew her out of existence. Thick brain matter exploded onto the man behind her. He looked normal, except his head was covered in slimy, rotted brain. His mouth opened and a distended tongue slopped out, licking at the old blood.

Gross.

I wanted Blaze to jump down once I'd lured the zombies away, but there was no time to verbalize the plan. Blaze was smart and I trusted she could figure it out for herself, so I spun around and jumped off the log, heading back into the forest.

A few glances behind me confirmed the zombies followed. I broke into a fast walk, because running was unnecessary. As long as they were behind me and I wasn't cut off, I could lead them around for a lifetime.

Rain dripped from leaves and pine needles, splashing onto my exposed skin as I led them along. All the combined scents of a forest washed out the usual smells of decay and apocalypse. (The scent of apocalypse, I discovered, was a mélange of oily smoke, rotted tissue, and general destruction. If dictionaries were ever revised, I was going to loan a hand in redefining the word.)

More rounds rang throughout the forest, this time from the direction of the auto shop. I took the cue as Blaze's signal for me to come out. Turning my attention from the slows, I became a runner.

Black and chipped teeth were at my eye-level, framed by blistered lips. The deceased corpse in front of me was over my height of 6'1." Intimidating would've described him as a living human, but paled in comparison to what he was now.

His hands shot out for my neck and he pulled me close to his putrid mouth. My shotgun pressed between us, its hilt stabbing into my chest and into his abdomen. I pulled the trigger, not seeking damage but a lapse in his concentration. He grunted and stumbled back, his hands lessening their grip. I took advantage and pumped the shotgun before delivering a buck shot straight into his head. His body cracked branches when it fell.

In the distance I could hear fast rustling through the forest, including savage howls from what could only be a pack of runners. They didn't know quite where I was, which gave me an advantage. If I could get out of the woods fast enough, Blaze and I could escape without any more difficulties.

Now that the undead behemoth was out of the way, I continued forth. A thicket of blackberry bushes lashed at my face, tearing open the scabbing wounds on one side and creating new ones on the other. I barely registered the pain. There was one place I needed to get to and nothing was stopping me.

Just when I began to think I was lost, I broke into the cement clearing. Blaze stood a few yards away from the Mustang, picking off runners emerging from the forest. Every time I heard a round of fire, a runner fell.

Panting, I slammed up against the Mustang, grasping for the handle.

"Took you long enough," Blaze called as she walked backward toward the car, shooting all the while.

I got the door open and was just about to slide in when I noticed a hand clenching my ankle.

Intestines trailed behind the torso that was gnawing on my steel-toed boot. Her face was torn into ragged bits, but her mouth worked just fine. In one swift movement, I yanked my foot back and brought it down on her skull, crushing it and breaking into the dead brain underneath.

I slammed my door shut and pressed the lock down, just for good measure.

"Get in!" I shouted, lunging for the driver's door and pushing it open.

Blaze turned around and tried to dive into the car, but a runner came out of nowhere, latched onto her, and fell. He looked like an undead hippie. Long, ratted brown hair straggled around his head. Blood coagulated in his rat's nest of a beard. An oversized tie-dye shirt completed the ensemble.

Despite the difficulty of yielding the shotgun in such close quarters, I brought it to his head and pulled.

Empty.

Still only half way in the car, Blaze tried to turn over and kick the zombie off, but she wasn't succeeding. I reached down in a flash, grabbing my 9mm, and squeezed the trigger.

A clean round went straight through his left eye. Blood splattered onto Blaze's camouflage jacket, soaking the middle of her back. I leaned over and shoved the body from the car, catching sight of a horde of runners headed straight for us.

Blaze shifted into place and closed her door, just as one of the undead slammed up against it. A hairline crack coated in blood appeared.

I punched her in the shoulder and yelled, "Get a fucking move on!"

"Don't get your panties in a bunch," she said as she turned the ignition. The blessed engine rumbled to life a second before she put the pedal to the metal.

The speed pushed me back into the seat. From the backseat, I heard a frantic mewling noise and claws on leather.

When this ends, I thought, I'm building a mansion for that ferret.

Blaze expertly drifted onto the empty highway and evened out her speed. I twisted around and saw at least fifteen undead curving around the corner of the body shop, rampaging toward us.

I wondered when they'd slow down and become a normal, pleasingly slow undead.

"Well, that was successful," Blaze said as she wiggled uncomfortably in her seat. I heard the wet sound of blood sliding against the hard leather behind her.

"Sure was."

I stole another glance behind us, only to see the Zs fading into the thick fog of morning.

"For a second back there, I thought you were going to sacrifice yourself for me."

Blaze chuckled, an amused grin curving her lips. "You thought that?"

It was hard to say whether I thought that or not. Recently words slipped from my mouth without me consciously deciding to say them. If I were going to get it together one of these days, I needed to work on that.

"No. I suppose not."

Chapter 22

An idyllic ten minutes of driving brought us to a hole-in-the-wall kind of town called Startup. I remembered seeing it on the map and thinking it was small, but not this small.

If Blaze hadn't slowed down as we entered, we could've passed through the entire town in less than a minute. But I didn't blame her. There were some sights to behold.

Grotesque, lopsided crosses lined both sides of the road and were planted in dead, brown grass. Decapitated bodies were nailed to them, crucified. No other whole bodies were to be seen, but thick mounds of gore were spread out in the grass and on the highway.

Memories of my time in Arkansas surfaced. The gruesome scene reminded me of time spent with Frank hunting and gutting deer. We would lay the bodies out on the dead grass in front of his cabin to skin them.

"This is the worst thing I've seen yet."

"I've seen worse," Blaze said as we slowly moved deeper into the tiny town.

A small gas station proclaiming "kegs to go" had black crosses spray painted on its side and the cement around it, along with a myriad of other graffiti.

Hell has come.

Ye shall be purified. We shall be purified.

God's doing.

My eyes stopped on one set of words in particular: *We are watching you.* I swallowed nervously. It wasn't like anyone was really watching me. So why was my hair standing up?

Drawing my eyes away from the gas station, I noticed a church to my left. It was old, with a steeple and everything. Metal structures were strewn about the front of the building, and a sign revealed it to be an antique store. Farther down the street were some houses and a post office, but I didn't want to stick around.

"Let's move."

Blaze nodded, not rushing as she lit a cigarette. Her lighter was red with a naked, voluptuous woman on the side. She caught me looking at it and winked.

"This one caught my eye at the gas station."

With an irritated sigh, I said, "Great. Let's go."

"Yeah, yeah. You should relax someti—"

I had been fixated on the signs to the right, but that didn't stop me from noticing movement behind us and to the left. Stiffs were coming out of buildings. They looked fresh. A naked woman had dark blue rings of bruises around her neck, the only markings on her. Her skin wasn't gray and still held tones of living flesh.

Before I could catalogue any more of their features, the car jerked forward. Blaze didn't waste any more time. Smoke pluming around her face, she eased on the gas and we escaped the undead with no issue.

We'd only gone a few yards when she slammed on the brakes, sending the car into a skidding stop.

"There's a blockage up ahead. Boards with nails. I don't know where to go. There's no turns."

"Let's just get out and move them, for fucks sake!"

Her voice rose in anger. "Look, you idiot."

I took the time and looked. There were two rows of boards, each extending off the road. The individual rows were two long pieces connected in the middle in a hinge fashion with a padlock. It became evident they could be unlocked and opened like gates.

More zombies shambled out of an antique store beyond the barriers, and were coming towards us. We didn't have enough time to figure out the mechanics of both barriers. The undead surrounding us were slow, but not slow enough.

I thought fast. Our options were narrowed to two solutions. We needed to get out of their sight so they could forget us. We needed to find somewhere to hide while the stiffs dispersed. While they did, we could form an exit strategy. The second, desperate plan was to run across the town and hope we made it to the Kellogg Lake Road in time. It sounded appealing, but we would have to leave everything behind. If the first plan didn't work out, we would fall back on the second.

"Get out of the car. If we take off, we can let them follow and leave the Mustang. We'll come back when it's clear."

My plan must've been decent—that or Blaze didn't have a better one—because she grabbed her gun from the backseat and got ready to follow. I did the same and opened the car door, ready to bolt, but first I reached into the back and grabbed my pack. It took three fast tries before I grabbed Pickle by the backside and shoved her into her spot in the backpack. There was no way to know where we'd be going or for how long.

Before getting out of the car, she turned it off and pocketed the keys. Blaze swiftly exited and set off in no particular direction. I slammed the door shut and followed her.

None of the buildings within immediate sight appeared to be formidable or even accessible. Most of the structures were thoroughly boarded up, not granting entry of any kind, or were destroyed beyond all reason.

After catching up with Blaze I said, "Let's get out of sight, first. They'll catch up, but it might confuse them."

She nodded and veered off to the right, behind a large square-shaped house. We trampled through tall, overgrown grass and entered an equally tangled backyard through an open wood gate. One lonely willow tree, half dead, loomed in the middle. The small backyard was cut off with a high fence. A single backdoor and window upstairs were on the back of the house. I shook the handle, expecting it to be locked. It was.

"We could circle back around. They're probably gone," Blaze said, slinking over to the gate and pulling it closed. It didn't look strong. The undead could easily bring it down if they tried hard enough.

"I doubt it. They were going berserk for us," I countered. "There's no way others wouldn't hear them and decide to join the party."

Blaze blew out a long breath and shrugged. "Then what?"

I opened my mouth to say something, but sounds came from inside the house. At first just scuffling, but louder sounds followed, like furniture being slid.

The door creaked open to reveal a sallow, fearful visage. It was a man—one who was probably a real big guy before he started starving to death.

"Get in," he said, pulling the door open farther. "Before someone sees you."

Not this again. Dealing with other survivors hadn't yielded anything good. On the other hand, we had nowhere to go. And if things started looking shady, we also had guns.

I moved forward and the man stepped aside, letting Blaze and me in.

The interior smelled and looked foul. The house appeared to be in the early stages of construction. No sheetrock had been laid, and only the skeletons of walls remained. It was dim, despite the two diamond-shaped lights up high on the left wall.

People of all ages and sizes were huddled in every available space. I counted ten before deciding to stop paying attention. This wasn't looking good. People who were in bad shape often wanted things from those who weren't.

Each of them turned their heads and peered at us, fright and confusion evident. Some of them started whispering the word "military" or "army." I guess they hadn't seen anyone as well outfitted as us and were getting the wrong impression.

The door closed behind us and I turned to look at the man, who I pegged as the leader.

"I'm Michael," he introduced, offering a dirty hand to me.

I bit my lip and looked at his hand, then back to him. Michael squeezed his hand shut and pulled it back to his side. Some people were too kind for their own good, Mike there being one of them. I wouldn't put it past him to try and save every human being on the earth if someone said he had a shot. He already had a good start, which was evident by the numerous survivors crowded around us.

"We'll only be staying a little while," I said. "No need for introductions."

Michael's face crumbled. A woman pushed past us and wrapped bone-thin arms around him. "You're cruel!" she hissed.

"No, Angie. It's fine." He sighed.

The woman broke away and pointed a finger at me. "You think you're staying for a little while? They know you're here. It's only a matter of time before they come to get us. All of us!"

I glanced at Blaze, who remained as blank as ever, then to Angie. "Who is going to get us?"

A haughty, pleased look crossed her face. "The lunatics down the street in the church."

"The antique store?"

Michael chimed in, "No, there's an old church across from the tennis court."

"They're the ones who started crucifying people," Angie said. "Not dead ones either, but us. They come when we least expect it and take us."

Someone in the room weakly added, "They don't always kill us."

Angie said, "They keep the girls and women. Sometimes we escape while they're taking us to the church."

Well, nothing new there. People kidnapping other people during an apocalypse to murder, rape, and otherwise disrespect. I didn't voice this observation to anyone, of course. No need to upset the natives.

"And you probably led them here. They have someone who watches from the antique store, then they signal the ones in the church."

I rubbed my temples. A headache was brewing already. Typically, I wasn't very perceptive of what people wanted, but in that instance I knew exactly what Michael, Angie, and all the other people wanted from us.

"You have guns," Michael said. "We don't have any way to defend ourselves. We're too weak."

Angie cut to the chase. "You can kill them so we can take the church back."

"Take it back?" Blaze said. "You must've had a dispute with them?"

Naturally they had to delve into a huge story.

When word of the Zs came to Startup, Washington, the entire town worked together to gather resources and fortify the big ol' church across from the tennis courts. Everything worked out for the hundreds of survivors until zombies actually came strolling into the town. People became polarized on who they thought should lead, what decisions they should make. And, as expected, some people went a little crazy.

Angie and Michael were married, and they led the half of the survivors who didn't agree with the crazy half. They wanted them to get it together or leave, which they wouldn't. Hence the murdering, crucifying, and general bad behavior.

Since they'd been kicked out weeks ago, the crazies had been tracking them down and killing them. None of them, Michael explained, had eaten anything substantial in a long time. They ventured from house to house when they thought it was safe and ate what they could.

There were a hundred of them in the beginning, and only forty were left.

After hearing their story, I wasn't moved. Surprised? I didn't feel outraged or too biased toward one side or the other. Actually, I was more eager to get out of there than anything else. I knew it wouldn't be that easy though.

"How about this? We give you some guns once we get back to our car, then you defend yourselves. We have some shotguns and rifles in the back, with ammo."

Michael and Angie looked at each other, exchanging silent dialogue. Angie glared at us and said, "You're condemning us to death."

"It's our fault?" I was about to say more when Michael reached out and touched my shoulder.

"Let's go upstairs to talk." He gestured towards the other survivors, who were getting riled up by our confrontation.

The upstairs wasn't boarded, and as we came up we saw another handful of people sitting away from the windows. At Angie's command they slinked away, squeezing in with the rest downstairs. We stayed towards the back of the house where our visibility from the outside was reduced.

Blaze, who picked her fights at the most random of times, stepped forward and into the shorter woman's space. Angie was at least a head shorter than her, and probably weighed eighty pounds less, too.

"You condemned yourselves to death when you decided to hole up in a church with other people. Didn't you consider the repercussions of cramped quarters and psychologically stressful situations?"

Angie opened her mouth to speak, but Blaze rammed right on, invading her personal space. "No, you didn't. And now, like the fucking commie you've become, you want us to ride in on our white horses to save you. I don't think so. We're alive because we aren't as fucking stupid as you are."

Michael wrapped his arm around the demoralized Angie, pulling her close to him. "I can see why you're still alive. You have no heart."

Blaze's mouth twitched, one corner turning up into a smirk. "Exactly."

I stepped in. "We're not doing more than giving you a few guns. There's no point in talking anymore."

"Fine," Angie said. "At least stay up here until we calm everyone down, then we'll come get you."

We agreed. As they walked down the stairs, I heard Blaze mutter, "Fucking commies," one last time.

* * *

A kid stood near the willow, partially shrouded in the opaque whiteness of fog. She had her back to me, but I'd seen what she looked like earlier when she was still shambling around.

Besides the vicious slit in her throat, she looked quite normal. Long brown hair, still in pigtails, lay against her back. She wore a pink shirt under denim overalls. Ropes were still wrapped tightly around her wrists. Evidence she was one of the crazies escaped victims. I'd been watching her for at least an hour.

I wasn't worried about looking out the back window. The willow tree blocked vision from the few buildings behind us, and since Blaze wasn't interested in conversation, I was left to make my own fun. Watching an undead child wasn't necessarily fun, but it was something mindless to do.

When we first went up there, while watching the backyard, a handful of zombies broke through the weak gate and shambled in. They banged on the wall and backdoor for a while, but as per the norm, left upon finding no lunch available.

The noise must've scared the survivors because neither Michael nor Angie had come up yet.

"She gone yet?" Blaze asked.

"No." I sighed. "I'm about ready to help her along."

Stiffly, I stretched out my legs. The hollow upstairs amplified the sound of my boots scuffing against the plywood floor. I pictured everyone downstairs cringing, thinking the crazies outside could hear it. How could they live like that? Rats, scurrying into dark corners whenever a threat presented itself. I'd rather die.

I checked on Pickle a few times, but didn't let her out. She seemed tired. When I pet her, I noticed her breathing was shallow. All the stress was piling up on her, but I couldn't help that. Every part of me wanted her to make it through this. Whenever I looked at her, I denied the possibility of her dying.

The sound of engines startled me from my dark thoughts. Shouts and movement outside followed the idling engines. I moved to the front windows, keeping my body to its side, and peered out.

A ring of men formed. They were faced away from the house, rifles pointed at the oncoming undead. Behind them was a smaller, inner ring of men scanning the perimeter. There were so many, they formed a fence from bodies. They picked off the Zs that drew too close.

To top it off, three ATVs waited with gun-toting men. Another six were visible, standing around near them. They formed a protective triangle around a big truck with a flatbed. Right below me, on the side of the house, four of them moved along the wall. The pleasant sunshine of late morning lit the entire scene.

These must have been the ex-followers Michael and Angie were going on about. They certainly looked crazy and on a mission.

I returned to Blaze. She looked up at me, and then ground her cigarette into the floor. In that flat, unmoved voice of her, she said, "We've got a problem."

Picking up my rifle, I slid out the clip. My wishing paid off. I had a full clip inside the carbine. To my dismay, my vest pockets yielded no more ammunition.

"Yeah. They're here," I said.

"I think we should just stay up here." Blaze sat up.

Downstairs we heard a few loud bangs, like knocking on a door.

"Why's that?"

"We know they want to come in and steal a few. They're *all* down there, and there's going to be a hell of a lot of chaos. They might not even come up here, especially since the upstairs looks abandoned."

I grinned. "Clever, Wright. Very clever."

She leaned against the wall, rifle in her hands. I did the same.

"You know what Gabe would've done if she were with us?"

Blaze shook her head. Her eyes flashed as she rolled them at me.

"She would've demanded we try to save them. It would've ended with the butt of my gun in her head," I said.

"You think too much, Cyrus. We just hang out up here and wait things out. If it ends without them coming up here, it's over with and we leave."

"Think too much? I don't think so."

"You should take up smoking." She pulled a carton from her jacket pocket then handed the silver and red Marlboro box to me, waggling her eyebrows. "Never too late to start."

Just to please her, I took the cigarettes and put them in my backpack. The idea of pleasing Blaze appealed to me. I wanted her recognition.

"They're coming in downstairs," she said. "Don't lose your cool."

Grinning, I replied, "Do I ever?"

The door gave way. A loud crash was followed by screams and scuffling. A yawning sense of guilt ebbed into my mind and I couldn't push it away. There were people downstairs that were going to—

Gunshots rang out. A bullet burst through the plywood a few feet away from us, sending dust and shards of wood everywhere. Downstairs the shrieks elevated. Commands were shouted, but I couldn't make anything out at first.

"Go upstairs…" "woman" "…camouflage."

My mouth went dry. I looked at Blaze, who frowned pensively and brought her rifle up, aiming it at the top of the staircase. They must've been watching us since we drove into town and left the Mustang.

Feet pounded up the stairs, bringing a flood of grimy survivors rushing for the corners. Blaze didn't open fire, but I followed suit and aimed as well.

Then a man wearing a ski mask, holding a shotgun, rushed up and in the room. I let Blaze take the shot, which she did with accuracy. The man's head jerked back and blood splattered onto the wood behind him. His heavy body thudded down the stairs, creating outraged shouts.

"We need to get out of here!" Blaze yelled. "Alternate route!"

I didn't like taking commands, but she was right, and a better shot than I. I assumed she would provide cover while I found another way out—which would be where, exactly?

While pushing skeletal figures out of my way, I ran to the window. My hopes were fulfilled. None of the men on the ATVs, or any others, were visible. They either went into the house or were somewhere else. Where they were, I didn't care. What mattered was the porch covering right underneath the window I was at. All I had to do was open the window, then Blaze and I could easily jump onto the roof and tumble off into the yard. It was only a ten foot drop, and we might get hurt, however…

What other option do we have? I thought. It's not like we can run downstairs. Who knew what the fuck was going on down there, or how many of the crazies were below rounding up people to take.

I flipped the tiny lock on the window and slid it open. Lucky for us, it opened to the side, which granted a lot more room for escape.

Blaze let off another round, and I spun around to find survivors and crazies alike pushing past each other to get upstairs. All the commotion reminded me of stirring old fruit and watching fruit flies spread out. I wasn't sure where her bullet went, but I shouted for her as I kicked the screen out and flung a leg over the windowsill.

Hot sunshine beating down on me, I stood on the roof ready to go. I slung the rifle on my back and shifted so I could help Blaze through.

Except she wasn't there. She was being dragged to the staircase by two beefy men. With great vigor she struggled, but the two thugs were taller and definitely heavier. She didn't have a chance.

Rage filled me as I clumsily climbed back through the window. The two saw me, clearly understanding my mission, and shouted for help.

In a swift movement, I released my 9mm from its holster and brought it up.

"Let her go, you fucker!"

They didn't reply, but kept moving toward the staircase. There were only five or six feet between us. Her captor's bloodshot eyes gleamed and his sweaty, thick hands clenched her arms.

I squeezed the trigger and a bullet soared right into the left one's shoulder, knocking him back. He let go of her, but they had already reached the staircase. Two more crazies showed up, dragging her down.

My emotions got the best of me and I couldn't see straight. I had to save her. I took aim and fired at the one coming toward me, but I only grazed his arm. Before I knew it, he had me on the ground, beating my face in.

Blood filled my mouth, and a second after that I saw stars. While they beat me to death, some of the fucking lunatics led Blaze away.

I didn't see things happening this way. Actually, I couldn't see anything at all after he smacked my head into the ground a final time.

Chapter 23

Nothing was worse than waking up from beating-induced unconsciousness. Well, I'm sure some things were worse, but at that moment, I couldn't think of anything that was.

Sticky, thick blood coated every crevice of my mouth. I inhaled and wheezed in pain at the tight feeling in my chest.

"He's waking up," someone whispered.

Just because I knew I had to, I cracked my less inflamed eye open and looked around. Dirty, frightened people stared back at me. They kept their distance, pressing up against the walls.

A face I knew hovered over me.

"They've taken two of us. A little girl and a woman," Angie said coldly. "They also took that woman who was with you."

Like I didn't already know.

Mentally bracing myself, I sat up. My back popped and cracked as I moved, stiff from being on the wood floor for so long.

"How long have I been out?"

Angie's eyes narrowed. "It's not like I keep track of time around here."

Michael came up the stairs and saw me, so I asked him instead. His forgiving, kind self smiled gently at me. "I'd say it's been at least two hours. You were still breathing, so we didn't worry."

I didn't say thanks. Instead, I stood up and looked around for my rifle. It was missing. So were my .40 and the 9mm.

"Where are my guns?"

Michael and Angie looked at each other, then to me. He said, "They took the rifle, but during the commotion Luke got the handguns and hid them."

"Hand them over, then."

Angie spoke up. "No. We're going to cut you a deal. Everyone go downstairs."

As obedient as well trained dogs, the survivors filtered downstairs, and in no time I was alone with Angie and Michael.

"We need you to do this for us. We're not strong enough or skilled enough."

At Angie's words, I gave Michael a blank look. I knew I wanted to get the fuck out of there and get Blaze back. What were they asking of me?

"We'll only give you the guns if you kill as many of the others as you can when you get your friend," Angie said, boldly stepping in and acting like she had an edge. I could tell she was disturbed by her own request.

I laughed then splayed my hands in front of her. "What did you think I was planning on doing? Negotiating?"

They looked at me oddly, then Michael turned away and walked downstairs. I heard talking, but didn't pay attention. Angie still stared at me.

"Do you have a problem?" I snapped. "We need to get this show on the road, sweetie."

"I can see why you've survived this long. You just don't care about anyone but yourself. That woman, your friend, she doesn't feel anything. That's why she's still around."

This chick would get along smashingly with Gabe, I thought.

"That's not true. I care about Blaze. That's why I'm going to get her."

Michael came up the stairs loudly, both my guns in hand. "We counted how much you have left while you were under. Both these clips are full, and you have two clips for each in your backpack."

They looked through my backpack? I was about to yell at them, but bit the inside of my lip instead and took the weapons away from him.

"I want you to know I'm not coming back here. I'm getting Blaze then we're leaving."

Angie's face went red and her fists closed into balls. "I figured as much."

"We'd like to thank you," Michael said, trying for strong but coming off as timid. "We need to be free from all this."

I shoved the .40 back in its holster, but kept out the 9mm. Without another word or wasted time, I marched down the stairs and out the door.

There I was, having to save someone yet again. Not just someone, but indirectly an entire group of people. I didn't want to come off as superior, but I was. Superior. If I wasn't, why were people chomping at the bit for me to save them?

Well, I wasn't sure if Blaze needed my help, but I assumed she did. If the crazies were worth their salt, they'd knock her out and tie her up. Together we could make it out. All I had to do was get to her and arm her.

I remembered Michael or Angie saying the church was across from the old tennis court down the street, but I decided to stop at the Mustang and retrieve a more formidable gun, first.

The backyard gate was off its hinges and the little girl by the willow was truly dead. Her little head was half missing from what I could tell, and her body was hidden in the tall grass for the most part. No undead were in the area, which made me think they followed the crazies out when they left. Unmoving corpses peppered the backyard and a broad radius in front of the house.

Sure enough, the front of the house was void of a fence or car of any kind. They were efficient when it came to unpacking and packing a kidnapping party. Down the street, my Mustang sat pretty and red, not to mention blissfully alone.

Fortunately, the door wasn't locked, because Blaze had the keys. When I got to it I jerked the door open, reaching in the back for a shotgun. It would do burst damage, which I'd need in the tight quarters of the church. I also took a .40 as backup. I rifled around for more ammunition, rushing in case an undead spotted me. I considered taking my pack off and leaving it, but I remembered the Hummer and decided to take it with. Someone could destroy, steal, or mangle the Mustang while I was gone. Then where would I be?

My back prickled, and I turned to see people staring out of the house I was just in. Angie was one of them, and two men behind her.

Shotgun in hand, I took a brief moment to assess the location of the tennis court.

The "tennis court" did not match its title. There was one tall fence still intact, with a few rotting corpses lashed to it. Grass grew in every crevice of the court, which was faded and cracked beyond use. Even its net was decrepit, torn and falling in most areas. The only reason I noticed it was because of the bodies. On either side of it were some baby cherry trees, creating even rows and a small amount of cover.

My vision went past them to the large, symmetrical building just beyond. The church had white siding that chipped away. There were evenly spaced windows on both the top and bottom stories, but the bottom ones were heavily boarded. Not wanting to stay in one place too long, I started off toward the left row of cherry trees, assessing the church all the while.

I had no way of knowing the best choice of entrance unless I circled the building and checked the other sides, which would take far too long. Instead, I opted for the lattice that was in the center of the building, with two two-story windows flanking it. Withered ivy would make it even easier to climb.

If I got up there, I could break a window and Rambo on in. No prisoners, no negotiations. In fact, no talking of any kind would occur. Just good old fashioned killing and rescuing. Saving a damsel in distress. I'd have to tell Blaze that one.

As I drew closer, I expected to be shot at or have an alarm to go off. None of that happened, which made me wonder what was going on inside. I ran from the trees and crossed a paved parking lot, my boots slapping against the ground too loudly for my liking.

Then I was up against the building, safe and sound. I looked out across the tennis court and saw a few corpses ambling out of whatever hiding places they came from, no doubt provoked by my noise and visibility.

There was no time to take care of them. By the time I got to the top of the lattice, they'd only be halfway across the tennis court, anyway. Unsure of where to put it, I shoved the shotgun into the back of my vest, wiggling it around until it seemed fairly secure. Not the cleverest of methods, but I wasn't going in there without it.

As predicted, the climb was quick and reasonably easy. I tried not to hit the wall while climbing. Surprise was the most important element. If someone knew I was out there, I was a sitting duck. A kid with a pistol could lean out a window and massacre me.

Once at the top, I paused and listened. There was no noise coming from the left window, but to the right there were clear wailing noises and some shouting. Moving sideways until I could just peek into the room, I leaned back and noticed the window was slightly ajar.

It was the reformatory in Monroe all over again. I could only see a small portion of the room where two women were tied to each other, and a little girl standing near them was also bound. The panicked women were gagged and shoved into the corner. Most of their clothes were in tatters, showing scabbed, bruised flesh underneath.

A cross was painted on the wall behind them, black and ragged.

Now I was closer, I heard the yelling clearly. It was a man shouting obscenities at the women.

The little girl turned and looked at me. I was only a few feet away from her, so I noticed when her green eyes grew wide. Hanging on to the lattice with one hand, I brought my other up and gave the universal sign for be quiet.

She almost nodded, but jerked her head toward the yelling, then said, "Take me. I'll go."

The man stopped yelling and silence followed.

Green-eyes turned her head slightly to look at me. I could tell she was trying to reassure me, and I wasn't sure why for a moment. Then it hit me. She was going to sacrifice herself somehow, probably so I could get in. How did she know I was on her side?

Maybe it was because I was hanging off the side of the house and not with the crazies, trying to kidnap or rape someone.

She walked out of my line of sight, but I heard her yell, "We're leaving!"

I was going to save that kid. Green-eyes was thinking ahead, giving me signals, and creating an in. She deserved to live.

A door slammed and the quiet remained prevalent. I shifted some more and reached for the window to pull it all the way up.

The two women closest jerked their heads toward me and started to fidget. They weren't as cool as the kid and might give me away.

Snatching my hand back, I tried to look non-threatening and took the risk of speaking. "Michael and Angie sent me."

That was a lie, but so what? They calmed down instantly and scooted away from the window. I lifted it all the way and brought my leg up so I could haul myself in.

There were a lot of them in there. I stood before at least twenty women shoved into a tiny Sunday school room. They were all tied up, some of them to each other, and some of them to a heater in the corner of the room. All eyes were on me, the pleading in their souls tangible.

Cyrus V. Sinclair. The V stands for valiant.

Having a conscience is terrible, I thought angrily as I moved to the closet group of ladies. *It really fucks you up.*

Even after I removed their gags, none of them spoke. Once their hands were untied, they set to work on the other women. In no time they were all freed.

"I'm looking for a woman. Tall, black hair, with a mean scar on her face. They just brought her here a few hours ago. Where is she?"

A middle-aged woman stepped forward, tears welling in her eyes. "Where they take the new ones. To…you know…"

My stomach tightened. I knew. I laced my voice with sympathy. "Where?"

"Down the hall. The white door. Please hurry. They just took Jenny."

I brought out my shotgun and pushed past all the women to the door. It was unlocked, which showed a definite lack of procedure on the crazies' part. It opened smoothly, revealing a man standing right across the hallway, a Playboy in hand.

This was the kind of guy who was going to rape Blaze. Beer-bellied, scraggly, and habitually fetid in nature. A delightful rage overtook me as I raised the shotgun and pulled the trigger. His head exploded, gore spraying in a beautiful 360 degree pattern on the stained wall behind him. As his body slumped down, I felt a giddy sense of triumph.

One glimpse told me the hallway led off down some stairs at one end and the white door waited at the other. Two more doors lined the hall, but both were barricaded. Midway toward the white door, a man tugged Jenny along. She went ballistic with screams.

He spun around when he heard the shot, fumbling for the pistol in his jeans pocket. Confusion and panic consumed him, and he shook too much to get the pistol out fast enough. I sprinted toward him, knocking him to the ground just as he retrieved it. The gun fell onto the tarnished wood floor, right next to little Jenny's feet.

Instead of wasting the ammo, I brought the butt of the shotgun down into the middle of his head. Again and again.

Blood burst from his face as I worked, one of my feet against his chest so the fucker couldn't get away.

Crack went his skull.

He wasn't getting away from me.

Burst went his brain.

He deserved to die.

When he stopped moving and screaming, I heard my pulse beating frantically. Jenny stared up at me, a spray of blood across her white-washed jeans near the shins. She reached down and picked up the pistol, opening her mouth to say something. Her words were cut off by the white door opening and the thundering of footsteps up the stairs.

"This might be it," I told her. "You and me, kiddo. We gotta cap these motherfuckers."

"Okay," came her weak, high-pitched reply.

A short man stood in front of me, a look of shock on his face. I looked past him and saw Blaze tied to a metal bed frame, unconscious. Her jacket was gone and she only wore the white undershirt I'd seen before. I focused on the man in front of me, just about to pull the trigger, when a little someone beat me to it.

The kickback on the pistol pushed Jenny into the wall, but her bullet hit him at an upward angle through the jaw. The top of his head flew off, blood and brain matter following his skullcap. The little girl slid down the wall, a blank look on her face.

Nothing was on my mind except getting Blaze. I took a step through the doorframe and tripped on a leg. There was a man to the right of the door, a baseball bat in hand. I fell partially onto Blaze, stirring her from unconsciousness. She opened her eyes and looked at me in shock.

Then I felt a heavy, wooden bat connect with the middle of my back. Pain jolted up and down my spine as I choked on the scream rising in my throat. My heavy tactical vest absorbed some of the impact, but not nearly enough. I rolled off of Blaze's legs as the man tried to grab me. Legs freed up, Blaze kicked him in the side of the head, her boot connecting solidly with his temple. He fell back against the door, shutting it.

Things were not looking good, and I was smart enough to admit it. Out of desperation, I grabbed the Glock, releasing it from its holster, and shoved it under the bed behind Blaze. I had to give her a chance, at least. The shotgun was just a few feet away in a pile of blankets. Although, they wouldn't suspect Blaze had a gun, and though she was still a bit groggy, I know she'd be alert soon.

Before I crawled to the shotgun two men burst through the doors, wielding hunting rifles. They weren't surprised to see me, and wasted no time in giving me a few sucker kicks before grabbing me and lugging me back down the hall. Blaze watched me go. The same man who hit me with the bat was up and out of the room, following the three of us as he went.

As they manhandled me out of the room, I couldn't find Jenny in the hallway. The door to the room with the women was also closed. Screwing my eyes shut, and having an unusual amount of hope in my heart, I wished for Jenny to keep on being helpful.

I was dragged through the bloody mess of the man I'd murdered with the shotgun. Thick, sticky blood drenched my hair and neck. The iron scent filled my nostrils.

"We got a special deal for you, buddy," one of the hulks said. "Oh yeah. We do."

We were at the stairs, and they kept on dragging. My body reeled in pain as I thudded down the stairs one at a time. The staircase was no longer than most, but it seemed infinitely long when pulled down it.

Once at the bottom, I noticed we were in the main congregation room. Corpses were nailed up on the walls and blood was everywhere. A putrid scent of urine and feces mixed with smoke made me gag.

The crazies had taken to lighting fires in metal barrels. Firelight danced on the walls, illuminating the repulsive figures nailed there. It was a regular old house of horrors, not like I was affected by that kind of crap anymore.

They stopped near one of the pews and jerked me around, tying me to the solid, wood bench. I tried struggling, but the pain in my back made my limbs numb.

"We're gonna be right back. We're gonna get Pastor North, and you're gonna get it."

Idle threats. I really didn't care. My head felt fuzzy. The two main doors were only barricaded with a big wooden slab that rested in slots, which meant I could escape through those. Hypothetically.

There were surprisingly few men inside the church. There were more than twenty back at the house, but now it seemed as though there were half that. And I'd killed two of them. Those that remained stood on the raised area behind the podium, where there were more pews and an organ, as though they were waiting for orders.

I heard a single round of a pistol go off, the one Jenny had, and my spirits lifted. There was no way to know if she fired the round, but I sure as hell hoped so.

A shotgun went off once, twice, from upstairs. Shouting started up again as well as screams of women. Rage filling me, I pulled at the ropes restraining me, wanting to get up there and get a piece of the action for myself. What I wanted more was to protect Blaze and not fail so miserably again.

A loud, splintering caught my attention. It was coming from one of the boarded windows on the wall opposite the staircase. An axe broke through, casting shards of sunlight into the giant room.

Somewhere near the front of the room, muffled voices and wood slammed against wood sounded.

Something was going on and I was completely defenseless.

The window gaped open and people began climbing through, some of them with guns and some with melee weapons. They were afraid, and some of them shook from the effort of climbing through. None of them saw me, as they congregated around the window. Michael hauled himself in, appearing confident, and I felt better about the situation at hand.

My restlessness grew and I bellowed for someone to untie me, but no one came. Those coming through the window were clearly filled with terror and incapable of fighting the better armed, better skilled lunatics.

I heard noise from the staircase and craned my neck to see who it was.

Blaze. Beatrice fucking Wright.

The front of her shirt was stained red with fresh blood. She took a few steps toward me, but stopped when she noticed what was going on, diving behind the pews across from mine. In her hand was the shotgun I had dropped. I looked past her and saw Jenny peek around the wall of the stairs. She grinned at me and waved the pistol.

She was a miracle if I ever saw one. She didn't need my saving—she could save herself.

Blaze's muscular arms twitched, then her whole body went into motion. She did a flawless dive across the aisle separating us and crashed up against me. She dropped the shotgun and tried to untie me. Sweat glistened on her forehead and her face was set in a deep grimace.

"Knife in my belt," I rasped. "Hurry."

Blaze finally located the knife and sliced through my bonds in a jiffy, then helped me move into a sitting position. She shoved the Mustang keys in my hands and pulled out the .40.

She said, "I'll cover you. We're leaving through the window."

I nodded, and adrenaline filled me to the brim again. Standing up, I caught a glimpse of the war. Survivors and crazies crouched behind pews, both sides taking potshots at each other. More of the church members came in from a side door and joined in shooting at Michael's people. I wasn't sure which side was winning, but a handful of survivors were on the ground bleeding and moaning.

The church was a deathtrap. People were dying, and it wasn't secure with the open door and broken windows. We had to get out.

I closed the distance between myself and the window and vaulted through it, hoping Blaze would make it, too. A second later she was out, and we were running around the church. Howls of the undead and screams of humans faded away the farther we ran. The tennis court teemed with slows, so we curved our path around them, making it to the blessed Mustang in no time.

"They opened the roadblocks when they took me," Blaze said.

"Good."

The Mustang went from stationary to fast in no time. Startup, and all of its problems, disappeared in my rearview window.

Chapter 24

"That worked out nicely." Blaze's voice sounded nasally from the blood still dripping from her nose. By the look of it, it might've been broken.

"Compared to what it could've been, yes."

The forest around us was bathed in golden sunlight. Between the time it took for me to wake up and the time it took to rescue her, hours had passed.

This is all coming to an end, I thought. *Kellogg Lake Road, the cabin, is minutes away.*

Just as I finished my thoughts, we drove past a yellow sign pointing to the very road. I let off the gas and slowed down, but Blaze touched my shoulder.

"Keep driving. They could drive after us, but if it looks like we're long gone, they might give up."

Nodding in agreement, I returned the car to a safe forty miles per hour, thankful the road was paved. They could've tracked our tire marks otherwise. My head and torso throbbed in pain, reminding me of the beating I sustained earlier. A profound lust for a bottle of painkillers overtook me. The craving itself almost hurt.

Her voice slithered in the dark car. "I wouldn't have left you."

I stole a glance at her. The golden hour revealed very slight red strands in her otherwise raven black hair. Bruises formed all over her face. Blood dried around her chin and nose.

Quickly turning my eyes back to the road, I replied, "Thanks, I guess."

We passed trees and the occasional house set back far from the highway. The setting felt so normal—just a drive in the pretty weather in a nice car. Indulging my newly recognized fantasy for normalcy, I basked in it.

I looked at her again, and she turned her head so that our eyes met. Blaze's lips curved up into a tiny smile. "You're not so bad, sometimes."

"Oh?"

She nodded. "I can't tolerate most people. In fact, I usually want to kill them. You're different though, so I like that."

I remembered back in Monroe when she asked if I was attracted to her. Though I tried to be indirect with my answer, I had a feeling she knew very well that I had the hots for her.

"I feel the same," I said, giddiness coming over me, accompanied with a lightness in my stomach.

"Just because I'm skilled and a better shot than you, doesn't mean…" She stared out the window then finished. "I don't know. This is all very foreign to me."

"What is?" I prodded, wanting something concrete from her.

"Don't act like you don't know. The apocalypse. It forces us to reevaluate ourselves and what we're willing to admit. I've never known how to talk about my feelings, so I certainly don't know how the fuck to do it now."

I laughed and took one hand off the steering wheel to pat her on the shoulder. "You're not alone, sweetheart. Do you think I find a suitable woman often?"

"Suitable woman?"

Our eyes met again and I reached up to touch her chin. "Suitable woman."

She smiled big enough to reveal her chipped canine. My hand fell away from her face and she turned away. "This is crazy. I never thought—"

The bridge up ahead was missing a huge section in its middle. Blown up. I had just enough time to view the giant, gaping hole one would typically drive over, and slam on the brakes, but it was all too late.

The Mustang flew right over the crumbling edge and into the rocky embankment on the side.

* * *

Somewhere in the distance, a frog croaked at even intervals, while crickets rubbed their legs together incessantly. Rushing water added to the mix, creating a symphony of natural music. Outside was bathed in a pleasant post-sunset light.

If every part of my body hadn't been vaguely tight or in excruciating pain, I would've taken time to appreciate the ambiance. I was slumped forward, head resting on the steering wheel, preventing me from any form of relaxation fitting to the music outside. The Mustang was at a downward angle, so my seatbelt dug painfully into my chest and stomach. Slowly, I became aware of the water that sloshed around in the car. My legs were soaked and cold.

The smell of gasoline and oil had been giving me a headache while I was asleep, and now that I was awake I could really appreciate it. Both of my temples were knotted and throbbing with red hot pain.

I raised my head just a tad and saw that the windshield was completely missing. An old log jutted from its center and into the car. Rotten vegetation coated it, some stray pieces floating in the Mustang.

Regardless of the pain and effort it took, I turned my head to see Blaze.

She wasn't there.

I glanced in the backseat, but saw nothing. Our weapons were gone, too. Angie and her people took all of them when they made their push against the crazies.

"Blaze?" My voice cracked and blended in with the sounds of the river.

She flew out of the car, I told myself. *That's what happened.*

As I unbuckled my seatbelt, I maneuvered into the back to retrieve anything of use. Pickle scampered around on the back window. I found and unzipped my backpack, leaning across the backseat so she could climb onto my arm, then into the safe, dry bag. She did so without hesitation, for which I was grateful. Any more difficulties and I'd have had a mental breakdown.

It was challenging, getting out of the car. My door was pressed closed by a huge rock, so I slithered out of the window and up onto the gravel bank. The rocks were moist and hot from the heat of the day. The warmth of them seeped through my ungloved hands as I slipped and grabbed, making slow progress upward.

Once I got up onto the crest of the slope, I glanced around. The other side of the river teemed with undead. They fell into the water in attempts to get to me, but the current on that side swept them away effortlessly, along with the contents of the Mustang's trunk, which had broken open, releasing all the food Blaze and I had gathered.

All that candy, gone. All the medicine, food, and water, gone. Collectively, I'd argue that my luck was fucking terrible. I couldn't hold on to items or people for more than a few days.

Gathering my wits, I began looking for her. I walked down the road and searched the ditches on either side, but she wasn't there. I even risked yelling until I was too nervous of the attention it would draw. Night was coming. My vision was degrading, but I kept looking until it wasn't safe to go on.

My head still hurt and my body ached until I could think of nothing else. I returned to the bridge, trying to form a plan as I hobbled along. I had to get back across the river and onto Kellogg. If Blaze was alive, she might've crossed it and went looking for the cabin.

The top structure of the bridge was still intact; only the cement was gone. I walked to the cutoff and studied it for a moment, before committing to a plan. If I waited long enough, all the stiffs on the other side would be gone, having jumped off the bridge, I could climb over the bridge to the other side. Kellogg Lake wasn't far from there.

My body screamed at me when I sat down on the hard road. Coming up with a thousand ways Blaze could still be alive would pass the time until I heard the last Z jump.

Then the sun went away, leaving me alone in the undead world.

Chapter 25

When I was twenty, I had a girlfriend. I'm not quite sure how it happened, but it did. At the time, I was living in a moderately sized town, teaching community Russian lessons three times a night.

I speak Russian—forgot to mention it. Seeing it's the most useless skill to have during a zombie apocalypse, why would I bring it up?

There was one girl, a blonde, who was always hanging around after class. She was my age, I imagined, but I honestly didn't care. I wasn't interested in her, but I could see why others might be. Nice complexion, a curvaceous body that was just shy of being on the skinny side.

She made quick progress in asking me on a date, which I declined immediately. But try after try, she came back. I figured saying yes would get this whole ordeal over with sooner rather than later.

I was mistaken.

Her name was Nicky and she decided she was my girlfriend, which meant calling me at odd hours and me paying repeatedly for dinner and movies. Had I known it was going to be that bad, I would've killed her to save myself the trouble.

It was all very funny. I felt as though I had accidentally gotten on the wrong train and had to see it through until it arrived at the next station. If anything, I was just along for the ride, and the scenery and entertainment were strange.

After a few months, I decided to end things while I still could. I managed to break myself out of the bizarre reality that was my life, and told her I wasn't interested in her anymore.

Not like I ever was to begin with.

Nicky practically had a psychotic breakdown when I told her. I wasn't a good judge of character. Less so back when than I am now, so it didn't register she'd been unusually obsessed with me. At the time, I had no clue why she was so dejected by the ending of our relationship. No idea at all.

The night was clear and cold. The moon was full and heavy in a sky speckled with thousands of stars. One last splash, followed by an absence of the music of the undead, told me the last of the Zs had fallen into the water. I got to my feet, taking the last bite of the Snickers bar, and dropped the wrapper off the bridge.

Remembering what was in my pocket, I withdrew a can of condensed milk from my pants. At least Judy-Beth did that much for me. With a thankful prayer in my heart for pop-top cans, I removed the lid and tossed it into the river. Not bothering with the formality of using my finger to scoop it out, I let the thick sugary concoction slide into my mouth.

Well, now I knew how Nicky felt. The gnawing sense of anxiety that ripped my insides up, accompanied by a wash of emptiness. My chest was so tight I felt like it might implode. I'm surprised Nicky didn't just kill herself. It felt so hideous

It hadn't taken long for the rest of the zombies to fall into the water. Maybe a half hour tops. They filtered through the woods and onto the highway, making their way to the bridge, before jumping off in attempt to get me.

Once half the sugar milk was gone, I dropped the rest into the river and licked my lips clean. My sweet tooth was sated, and it took the edge off my misery.

After shaking my limbs out to relieve the numbness from sitting, I set to work on traversing the bridge. Its structure allowed for easy climbing, and the work became mindless.

I was still in shock and I knew it. In fact, I embraced the sense of emptiness that was keeping me sane. Blaze meant something to me, and my mind was protecting me from an inevitable breakdown. It was smart and knew to wait until I was safe. I dreaded the moment when I'd realize it was entirely my fault she was dead or alone. How could I live with that?

Shocked, I stopped a third of the way across the bridge. Suicide was an option I hadn't considered before, and it was one that made sense. One bullet, right then, and I wouldn't have to worry about getting to the cabin or anything thereafter.

Shame washed over me and I began moving again. Suicide was a big copout. Besides, what would Pickle do without me? I owed it to her not to do it. Blaze wouldn't have done it, either. If she were still alive and I mentioned the idea to her, she would've called me something derogatory and lit up a cigarette. I ran through a dialogue in my mind, in an attempt to lighten my mood.

I think I should kill myself.

You would think that, you cocksucker.

No, really.

Well, go ahead. I certainly won't stop you, you panty wearing fuck.

I laughed sadly. Making up conversations between us wasn't going to help my mental state in the least.

Only ten minutes later, I landed on the other side of the bridge, a barely lit expanse of highway before me. After I attempted to clear my mind, I started the jog to Kellogg Lake Road.

* * *

No one was waiting for me. The town of Startup was entirely visible in the moonlight, but seemed as empty as it had been when I first arrived. I didn't hesitate to make the right onto Kellogg, not interested in investigating that forsaken town again.

The trees closed in overhead, blocking out a majority of the light. I would've been afraid if I wasn't so deadened already. Fearlessly, I continued my jog up a large hill, paying attention for the markers Frank explained would get me to the cabin.

* * *

A few hours later, I stopped at an abandoned double-wide trailer for the night. When I woke up, I fed Pickle some cat food I found in the kitchen.

I lost it there. I sobbed until my eyes felt fiery and my throat hurt. Blaze's face wouldn't leave me. When I closed my eyes that's all I saw. I punished myself for what happened to Frank, Blaze, and Gabe. The burden of their lives weighed down my entire being. My episode went on for hours until I forced myself to even out and focus only on surviving.

When I got my act together, I left.

All day I walked or jogged until I found the first of Frank's signs: a yellow, steel roadblock. It opened up into a gravel area where a small electrical substation was fenced in. Normally I'd hear a static buzzing of the transformers overhead, but everything was quiet as it had been.

I searched the perimeter until I found the first "F" marked tree, indicating the direction I should go. It was like connecting the dots to find my trail. Once I found it I started the hike, following every clue Frank mentioned in his death-plagued delirium.

* * *

I hiked for days. I wasn't a decent mountaineer, so it took far longer than projected. No undead pestered me on the way; my location was so remote, it seemed impossible for even one of them to come shambling along.

On the second day, I ran out of food, and resorted to eating copious amounts of blackberries and huckleberries. Oh, I wished hard for some kind of animal to come along, but none did. I encountered plenty of streams along the way, so hydration wasn't an issue. Near one of the bigger rivers I even took the time to shower in a deep swimming hole I found.

It was hard to find the marked trees. Sometimes neighboring bushes were overgrown and covered the signs, or the trees had fallen, which added length to my trip. Each time I stopped to search tree after tree it added one, maybe two hours.

But then I found it. The cabin. First I found the edge of a tall chain link fence. Emptiness was so prevalent inside me, I couldn't muster up any excitement when I arrived at a gate, which had a padlock painted blue.

With shaking hands, I shrugged off my backpack and fished out the keys. I inserted the blue one, pulled the lock off, and pushed the gate.

It opened. I had arrived.

* * *

As I searched the compound, I realized the memory of my journey was shrouded in fog. It seemed like a hallucination. I shut down so I wouldn't think of Blaze, but that action seemed to have shut down the rest of me, too. I didn't mind.

Francis J. Bordeaux's cabin wasn't just a cabin—it was also a bizarrely advanced tree house. One large cabin was formed around a giant maple tree that seemed misplaced in the forest consisting mostly of pines and firs. A short distance away from the main cabin was a smaller one made of tin that housed the entrance to a formidably sized well.

His little compound was at the foot of a rocky cliff I estimated to be about a hundred feet up. The fence provided a good perimeter, both ends stopping at the cliff.

What was most spectacular was the hatch on the cabin ceiling that opened up to a ladder, which led up into the maple and into a grand tree house. It seemed like a safe house, or a last resort; all it had was a bed and a few other necessities. Two ropes led off the tree house platform. One led up to the top of the cliff and was tied to a tree, while the other lead to a pine outside the fence perimeter.

It was perfect when it came to survival. A slightly overgrown garden near the cabin produced corn—which meant it was late August—beans, tomatoes, and quite a few other vegetables. I didn't want to live on candy, MREs, and canned goods (which he had plenty of) forever, and was grateful for it.

Frank even had a collection of books on gardening, property maintenance, and other useful volumes in the lower cabin.

My location, physical health, and resources were perfect. The only thing damaged, quite honestly, was my heart.

But I survived, and that's what mattered. Maybe my chi would realign and I'd be the apathetic motherfucker I was when this all started. That would certainly be easier, wouldn't it?

I looked out into the vastness of the forest and sighed.

My name is Cyrus V. Sinclair. The V stands for—

Well, it doesn't matter anymore, now does it?

Epilogue

Cyrus V. Sinclair leaned back in a comfortable, but ugly, recliner. Warm, golden rays of sunshine filtered in through the wooden slats of the window and onto the smooth oak floor. Birds tweeted outside, having a lovely time in the late October weather.

He was finally alone. He was glad to be alone. During the first few weeks of solitude he had endured a bad case of cabin fever, but it passed. Now he spent the days tending to his compound and gardening.

No one could see him, but he grinned sheepishly. Gardening was the last thing one would expect from Cyrus, but every day he'd go out and work on his year-round garden. Everything had settled down and he was alone again.

For reasons unknown to him, especially under these ideal circumstances, Cyrus's throat tightened and he choked back a sob.

He was alone again.

Frank was dead because Cyrus couldn't think clearly. Blaze was probably dead because he wasn't paying attention. And Gabriella…she was gone and almost certainly dead because she needed him to take care of her, to be there, and he wasn't.

A wet, foreign substance rolled down his cheeks. Angry at himself for such a display, he went to wipe the tears away, determined to stop his crying. He stood up on quavering legs and went to the small wooden dresser standing near his bed. He opened the top drawer and pulled out the box of cigarettes Blaze had given him in Startup.

It's never too late to start.

That meant a lot, now. He drew one cigarette out and set out to find a match. While he looked, he considered every meaning of that sentence. It was never too late to learn to love someone.

It was never too late to grow a conscience.

* * *

When Blaze opened her eyes, the sun was setting. The distant sound of zombies made her pulse speed up. Her entire head felt like a batter had used it as a baseball and really, really didn't hold back.

She didn't know where she was or why she was there. The bridge breaking, the crash. The nothingness. It was a blur. Blaze tried standing twice before succeeding on the third try.

They were standing across the broken bridge, some distance away. She was forgetting something, but she had no clue what it was. Blaze patted her pockets and found nothing but a crushed lighter and her hunting knife. No gun.

Was she with someone?

How did she get there?

Had she been driving?

Her head swam and she stumbled forward. The yellow markings on the road doubled. She couldn't remember anything, but she knew she had to find somewhere safe to stay until her head stopped buzzing.

A dazed and confused Blaze Wright slowly walked away.

About Eloise J. Knapp

Eloise J. Knapp currently resides in Washington state, where *The Undead Situation* is based, and is working on a degree in graphic design. *The Undead* Situation is her first novel, and she is currently working on the sequel

Knapp both took the photo and designed *The Undead Situation*'s cover. Her other published graphics include the first *Metagame* cover (by Sam Landstrom), and the photo for *Jumping off Swings* by Jo Knowles. Landstrom is the cover model for *The Undead Situation*, depicting the main character Cyrus V. Sinclair.

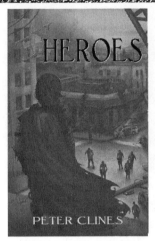
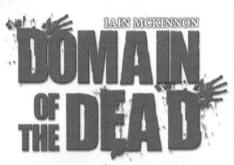

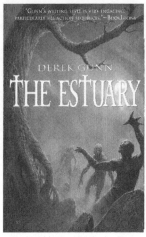

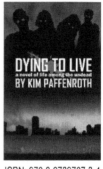
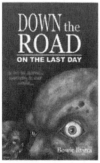

BY WILLIAM D. CARL

Beneath the dim light of a full moon, the population of Cincinnati mutates into huge, snarling monsters that devour everyone they see, acting upon their most base and bestial desires. Planes fall from the sky. Highways are clogged with abandoned cars, and buildings explode and topple. The city burns.

Only four people are immune to the metamorphosis——a smooth-talking thief who maintains the code of the Old West, an African-American bank teller who has struggled her entire life to emerge unscathed from the ghetto, a wealthy middle-aged housewife who finds everything she once believed to be a lie, and a teen-aged runaway turning tricks for food.

Somehow, these survivors must discover what caused this apocalypse and stop it from spreading. In their way is not only a city of beasts at night, but, in the daylight hours, the same monsters returned to human form, many driven insane by atrocities committed against friends and families.

Now another night is fast approaching. And once again the moon will be full.

ISBN: 978-1934861042

EDEN
A ZOMBIE NOVEL BY TONY MONCHINSKI

Seemingly overnight the world transforms into a barren wasteland ravaged by plague and overrun by hordes of flesh-eating zombies. A small band of desperate men and women stand their ground in a fortified compound in what had been Queens, New York. They've named their sanctuary Eden.

Harris—the unusual honest man in this dead world—races against time to solve a murder while maintaining his own humanity. Because the danger posed by the dead and diseased mass clawing at Eden's walls pales in comparison to the deceit and treachery Harris faces within.

ISBN: 978-1934861172

MORE DETAILS, EXCERPTS, AND PURCHASE INFORMATION AT
www.permutedpress.com

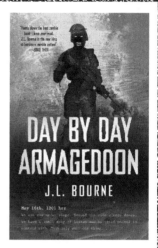

14212231R00134

Made in the USA
Charleston, SC
27 August 2012